Craig Jordan-Baker has published fiction in New Writing, Text, Firefly Magazine, Potluck and in the époque press é-zine. His drama has been widely performed in the UK, including his adaptation of Beowulf and he has had dramatic work commissioned from The National Archives, The Booth Museum of Natural History and the Theatre Royal Brighton. Craig lives in Brighton and is a Senior Lecturer in Creative Writing at the University of Brighton.

The Nacullians is Craig's debut novel.

THE
NACULLIANS

CRAIG JORDAN-BAKER

époque press

Published by **époque press** in 2020
www.epoquepress.com

Typeset in Brandon Grotesque Regular/Bold
by **Ten Storeys**®

Printed and bound in Great Britain
by Clays Ltd, Elcograf S.p.A.

British Library Cataloguing-in-Publication Data
A catalogue record for this book is available from
the British Library.

ISBN 978-1-9998960-7-2 (Paperback edition)

Mother

'That passed over, this can too.'
-Deor's Lament

THE
NACULLIANS

CHAPTER ONE

The Death of Patrice Nacullian
(1999)

What is about to come involves people who live in a house made of brick.

You might feel that to write of people in a house made of brick is a soggy submission to the everyday. Not so. It will be shown that such a tawdry setting hides qualities that are amusing and even enlightening, so I beg your patience.

This brick house was a brick house in a southern city and was a brick house on an estate in the east of that city. Three generations of the same family lived there and if such a thing seems unlikely, please remember that this was the twentieth century, a time when people lived together in wonderful and uninterrupted harmony. This family was founded by Patrice and Nandad Nacullian, who crossed the waters from another island sometime after the Second World War, to help rebuild a country they were at best ambivalent towards. Patrice Nacullian concentrated on pregnancy, smoking and crosswords, while Nandad spent his days laying bricks and being racially abused on building sites. That of course was until the blacks came along, after which time Nandad Nacullian may as well have been Winston Churchill or Queen

Victoria, he was considered so much like his English workmates.

Patrice and Nandad had four children: Niall, Betty, Shannon and Bernard. Niall died in the General Hospital when he was two hours old from a lung defect that stumped the doctors and in her sixteenth year, Betty died suddenly, from suicide. After this, only Bernard and Shannon were left, but the brick house remained the same brick house in a line of other brick houses.

It was not long before Bernard, promising fellow that he was, became a builder's apprentice at the same firm as his father. Bernard soon fell prey to the wonderful sense of belonging that comes from racial abuse and smoking rollups. He tormented a Trinidadian guy by the name of Christian Lovejoy to such a degree that one day, Christian left a dogshit in Bernard's hardhat. Bernard 'shithead' Nacullian was quickly renamed amid general mirth, but they all beat Christian terribly anyway and left him in the shell of the new shopping centre. Everyone claimed he must have been drunk and must have slipped on a girder.

This leaves us with Shannon, who, after getting pregnant by the local chip shop owner, decided to retire to the bosom of the family home. The owner of the chip shop, James Radley, already had a wife and two children, so had no intention of acknowledging the newest outpouring of his fecund loins. Patrice was shocked as much by her daughter's stupidity as by the general shame that came from the assumption that her Shannon was a whore, temptress, liar or fantasist. On the day Shannon's son Greg was born in the General, Patrice looked down at the lymphy damp little thing that had just emerged from her daughter, and she was wistful. Her own long-departed little boy was upon her at that moment and crossing herself, she swore to protect her grandson, bastard or not. Amid all the family drama that was to follow,

Nandad Nacullian made it his habit to sit in his green battered armchair behind the fortress of his daily paper, occasionally peering over its crenulations to ask for tea or that the radio be switched on.

This was until the mid-nineties, a time when Nandad became perplexed by the appearance of a third testicle in his ballsack. Initially, he looked upon this addition with vague suspicion, but eventually this suspicion gave way to a stolid and manly pride. You can imagine his embarrassment then, when after startling pangs of agony and months of malaise, he was told he had only weeks to live. He died five days after the prognosis, as much from awkwardness as the virulence of his cancer.

This left Patrice, Bernard, Shannon and Greg in the brick house on Harefield estate. At this point, your narrator recognises the need to move forward a couple of years or so, as very little changed in that house, aside from the dog passing away and milk delivery becoming less and less popular. You might say that time during this period was like a saveloy under a chip shop heat-lamp, close to closing time. That is, life looked pretty much as it always had, but it was somehow less appetising.

The saveloy analogy stops in 1999, just after breakfast. One day in this year, Patrice Nacullian announced she was bored with life and couldn't stand the thought of living into the twenty-first century, with all its things and all its stuff. There were enough things and stuff here in the peace and harmony of the twentieth century and she would be buggered, she said, if she would tolerate more things and stuff. All her life, she said, all her life she had seen an ever-increasing mountain of things and stuff piling up in the back garden of existence and she had had enough. Therefore, and with a definitive bob of her curly grey mane, she was resolved to die that evening in bed, after she had finished her customary cocoa and crossword.

Now the family, aware of Patrice's lifelong Catholicism and the Papal injunction against ending your own sorry time on this planet, questioned whether such a move meant suicide. If such a move did mean suicide, how was it that she could square this with her creator, who did after all grant her the good fortune of life and free will? But Patrice would have none of it and waved away the suggestion like she waved away the ever-hopeful attempts of Mrs Winter, the Avon lady, to ply her with creams and cosmetics, ever more bloody things and stuff. For Patrice did not intend to starve, overdose, hang, shoot, lacerate, immolate, eviscerate, suffocate or in any other way cause herself harm that would invalidate the sacred bond she shared with the Almighty.

'It will happen,' she said with another bob of her grey mane, 'as God intended.'

What this meant was at the time of speaking, a mystery. Still, back in the wonderful uninterrupted harmony of the twentieth century, people still had respect for their elders, so no one moved to question the solemn pronouncement. That night, which was a Tuesday, Patrice Nacullian made faggots and gravy with mash, which the family ate in habitual silence around the small table in the lino-floored kitchen. Bernard had recently come home from a day on the building site and was further-gone than usual. So much so in fact, that he slipped off his chair twice before vomiting into his mash with one almighty and manly heave. Patrice silently shook her head at him as he spat his apologies through chunks of stomach-lining and gestured to Greg to help him get upstairs. With a wince, Greg obeyed, if only because he wanted to get back to his meal as quickly as possible.

4

'Can I have the stuff without vomit on?' he asked Shannon on his return to the kitchen.

This was in fact the precise point where Patrice made her speech about things and stuff, and her intention that this night be her last. It was also a fact that this was when Shannon questioned the theological validity of her decision and whether it amounted to suicide or not, to which the old woman replied:

'It will happen as God intended.'

Like faggots and mash, this phrase was beyond familiar to Shannon, who heard this from her mother whenever something mildly upsetting came along. When the Labour landslide of 1997 threatened a descent into Godless communism, Patrice Nacullian said that it would happen as God intended. When Bernard was up in court for GBH on Christian Lovejoy, the outcome was to be decided as God intended and when Shannon first told her mother that she was pregnant by James Radley, the chip shop owner, Patrice shook her head and then said:

'It will happen as God intended.'

This reliance on a single phrase throughout her life left those around her unmoved, for like death threats, antibiotics and the National Anthem, things used all the time cease to be effective. Later, as she rinsed the vomit and gravy from the dinner plates, Shannon wondered what life without her mother would be like. With a lukewarm sense of deja-vu, she realised she had no idea whatsoever.

'Did you leave your uncle Bernard on his side?' Shannon asked Greg, who was slumped facing his Nan at the kitchen table.

'Yes Mum.'

'Good. Isn't it your turn to do the drying up?' Shannon asked her son.

'No! It's Uncle Bernard's.'

'So, I'll just do it my fucking self then, shall I?'

Then, like the forming of the Himalayas as a result of the meeting between the Indo-Australian and the Eurasian plates, Greg unfolded his arms, rose up from the table and stepped towards the kitchen sink.

As she digested her faggots, Patrice eyed the backs of her descendants whilst they begrudgingly worked amid the post-prandial steam and bubbles. She was aware that the pronouncement of her end had had little effect on those around her, and this was something of a surprise, as what could be more dramatic than death? It was all because people were too focussed on things and stuff, she thought. Patrice gazed upward to the kitchen's yellowy artexed ceiling, searching for God. In a small curved ruck between the lampshade and the doorway to the living room, she found him. She paused. She looked again at the backs of her daughter and grandson. And then she said something she thought she never would.

'You remember that James Radley, Shannon?'

Shannon's water-wrinkled, soapy hands stopped.

'I said James Radley. You remember him?'

Greg turned quizzically to consider his mother's sudden lack of composure.

'What?' said Shannon.

'Ye deaf, daughter of mine? I'm sayin' to ye, do ye remember that James. Radley?'

A spasm of bubbled water.

Shannon turned her head slightly. 'Owned the chippy down the hill yonks ago,' she spat and returned to her washing up.

'Yes, that's him. He's the one that gave ye Greg, didn't he?'

'What?' said Shannon.

'What?' said Greg, and he dropped his gingham tea towel on the chequered lino floor.

Patrice Nacullian felt the warm thrill of success run through her. 'James Radley, there you go. He's yer Daddy so he is, Greg. And a fuckin' cunt of a man if God Almighty'll excuse me for saying so.'

'Mum!' shouted Shannon.

'Mum!' shouted Greg.

And then there was silence.

'And now, if you'll excuse me, I'm going to get ready for me bed. Greg, would ye bring up me cocoa in about a half hour love?'

Greg's head moved upwards and then downwards several times. Shannon's wet hands dripped onto the lino.

A little over an hour later, the lights went out for the evening in the brick house in the east of the city. Those that slumbered, slumbered, those in fever, fevered. Those who were awake, were awake. Outside, the Solent bled into the English Channel. By midnight, Patrice Nacullian was dead.

This then is the end, or at least one of them. There are a several more ends to come and I should tell you now that they involve people who live in a house made of brick.

CHAPTER TWO

English Bond
(2012)

This is not a story, because lives are not stories, no matter what narrators claim. Lives have no ends that end in the proportioned and cemented way of stories. Neither do they have middles for that matter, and the beginning of a life is nothing more than a darkened window, which takes years to brighten. This is not a story, because this is about a life and if at any point this becomes a story, then take it that your narrator has failed you.

It was the home. 'The ancestral pile,' Bernard would jokingly call it. He was a stupid man and a mean man and this narrator would have had nothing to do with him if it were not for the fact Bernard Nacullian was part of the family. And we all know that families are impossible to ignore, whatever we think of them.

Bernard's joke was based on the fact that the ancestral pile was neither particularly ancestral, nor was it particularly pile-like. It was a small former council house in Harefield, hoovered-up for next to nothing when the government insisted on washing its hands of the national housing stock. In the future, when Bernard was dead, it would be snapped-up in a by-to-let frenzy and rented out to two families of Somalian immigrants for £4000 a month.

The landlords would make a handsome profit, and the kids of the Somalian immigrants would grow up to become gardeners, civic planners, shop-assistants, bums, graduates, addicts and narrators.

As his father had done, Bernard entered the building trade, much like a fly enters the dead anus of an urban fox: Some things follow by sovereignty of nature. He worked first as a labourer before moving on to groundwork and eventually, rose to become a mediocre bricklayer. Although he held no passion for the job, he could tell a stretcher bond from an English bond, a Dutch bond from a Flemish bond. He boasted he could read brick walls like librarians could read books, which was lucky, his co-workers joshed, because you can hardly read a fucking book yourself, can you, Bernard mush? He would redden at this and start at another roll-up to shut out the jeering. In his heart, Bernard felt he was always the butt of jokes and that this was unfair, though the word unfair had a childish ring, and Bernard would never speak it.

Bernard though was fond of some words, and perhaps his favourite was the word Nig-Nog. He thought about this word constantly, it was the ticking clock of his consciousness. Nig-Nog, Nig-Nog, Nig. The word was for him the perfect mix of a hallowed past where it was still permissible to say such things and a present where to say such things was to mark yourself out as outrageous; a prick certainly, but outrageous nonetheless. In truth he rarely used the word, and even when he did, it was a mumble or a gargled curse, for the man was not brave about his racism, though he was convinced that he was.

As well as his favourite word, Bernard had his favourite man, a singer who found fame singing patriotic songs about the fact you weren't allowed to say black coffee anymore due to restrictions on freedom of speech. And with these two things Bernard's life was complete. A man with a favourite word and a favourite man was a real kind of man. Like men who liked the word 'sundown' and John Wayne or the word 'escape' and James Bond. It was a diet simple and complete.

Now then, if a story is a wall, then the backstory is the foundation of that wall. And if a wall is also a metaphor, then a wall is not a wall at all, but a drawing of one, or perhaps an out-of-focus photograph of one, I'm not too sure. Not that this story is a wall, mind you. Anyway, I think that now the foundations are finished. But I'm less sure about the metaphor, or the drawing or the photograph of the wall. Still, I'm sure you can understand what I mean as well as a librarian can read a book, or Bernard Nacullian can read brick walls.

This house he called the ancestral pile was the house he was brought up in, the house he had shared with his siblings, the house he had lived in as an adult and the house his parents had died in. And finally, by force of time and regularity, it had become Bernard's. In the early noughties he had shared the space with his sister Shannon and her lardy, probably-poof son, Greg. But after their mother's passing, Shannon had itched to move on and take Greg with her, and so they did. There was never any question of Bernard paying Shannon her share of the property and she never asked, which was just as well.

He sometimes saw his sister while picking up a few bits on Bitterne High Street or when she came round with presents at Christmas. They always said they should meet up for a meal or a coffee sometime or maybe just a chat on the phone. It always seemed to them that they could never fully drop out of each other's lives, so effort wasn't strictly necessary.

Recently though she had been in hospital, a stroke, a stroke and a fall, and Bernard had stayed away, thinking she had her son after all, and he'd only be an intrusion. This was a lie of course, as he wouldn't have been an intrusion at all. But admitting he was scared his sister could die, was scared to maybe see her die, was something he would not do. He sent some chocolates though.

After Shannon and Greg had left the house back in 2000, it had suddenly seemed larger somehow, though a house is a house is a house, Bernard told himself. As a builder himself, of course he knew that a house was a house and nothing else. It was a stretcher bond house and a sturdy house and a cheap house in Harefield, and this was all.

But even if this was all, Bernard felt awkward about the ancestral pile. He never invited his workmates back because he understood that in its way, the house was creepy: it was a woman's house. It was a woman's house and either by laziness or nostalgia, or something unadmittable, Bernard would not change it. The house had floral tea towels and chequered lino and cups on hooks and ornaments of farmers and inherited pottery and pictures in the toilet and a white serving hatch and a Leyland cypress and a pond and a bird feeder frequented by sparrows. But despite being a woman's house it was just a house, though a house that seemed terribly large with the absence of women.

But neither would he allow women to enter either, so while Bernard desired fucks and intimacy like anybody else, the embargo generally prevented both. Sometimes when he imagined the scenario, he saw his one-night stand stepping over the threshold and the lights being snapped on. Before her was a museum of stained tea towels and chipped pottery and greasy lino and empty birdfeeders. In his imagination, she would ask him if his mother was out that night or maybe, with a smile, he was looking for someone to start work immediately? The smile would become a grin then and a laugh then and then her lipstick would be red and her hair would be in curls. And then, in his imagination, Bernard would hit her to the floor and the fantasy would begin to mist away as she dialled 999, telling him you're fucking dead meat, you cunt.

No, Bernard never had one-night stands.

It was a Friday night in Bitterne, a suburb of the city, and Bernard was drinking in his local, The Garden Wall. Friday night on Bitterne High Street is pretty much the same Friday night as every other Friday night before this Friday night, and back and back until the first of all Friday nights, the first of all Friday nights in those everywheres that aren't really anywhere at all.

The Garden Wall was a palace of TVs and fizzy beer. It had never closed, but always seemed to be changing hands, as if it was only ever able to break even. In the brown-beige back bar, a woman with an acoustic guitar was singing 'I Want to Know what Love is' to a small swaying audience of the totally fucked. It was a usual Friday.

Though for Bernard it was an unusual Friday. In the booze-damp beer garden, within the confines of its well-built masonry walls, he was snogging a woman and a woman was snogging him. He was groping a woman and she was groping him. He was dry-humping a woman and she was dry-humping him. Their torsos and hands moved over and around one another like practicing mime artists.

The woman had red lipstick and her hair was in curls, but

Bernard did not consider that this might just have been his imagination. With a little spasm, they emerged out of one another for a moment, to catch their breaths and swig at their drinks. Then the woman said:

'Do you think we can we go back to your place?'

Bernard began the transition from hard to semi-hard.

'But, what about your place?'

The woman frowned. Her red lipstick was red.

'Wife at home, is she?'

'No, no...I don't...it's just you might be...thought you might prefer...why not your place?'

The woman paused for a moment, eyeing her dubious conquest. 'Well, I asked first. God, whatever happened to ladies first?' she snapped.

Bernard went from semi-hard to not-hard, for he hadn't considered this. Yes, whatever had happened to ladies first? It was the thin end of the wedge, wasn't it? Ladies first had gone the way of Nig-Nog and of integrity in football and of small houses feeling small. No, he thought, she had asked first, and he had nothing to hide and the small house really was small, even if it didn't feel that way. He nodded and then reached for his phone, though his member retracted a little further, like a retired emotion.

Bernard did not tip the Somali taxi driver, who wasn't really a Somali, but a Tamil who had once been raped by a Sri Lankan army officer in a canvas tent, far, far away from this city.

The taxi puttered off down the road while Bernard and the

woman (fuck, what was her name?) stood before the ancestral pile. The place was dark. The woman tottered and guffawed as she walked up the short gravel driveway, past the cypress. She was feeling Bernard's arse like she was kneading dough, and this convinced Bernard that this could not be his imagination, because he would never have imagined a woman feeling his arse. Then again, he never thought he would have a fantasy where a woman phoned the police on him or called him a cunt, so he was less sure.

Around about now, you might think I'm wrong, because I stated that Bernard Nacullian never had one-night stands. But listen, the woman moved in six weeks later and by this time Bernard knew her name. Emily, Emily Header. She was a wry woman and a canny woman and this narrator would have had more to do with her, if it were not for the fact that Emily Header never became part of the family.

One night, three months after moving in and buying new tea towels, ripping up the chequered lino, stocking the birdfeeder and taking down the pictures in the toilet, Bernard hit Emily Header to the floor. If it was because of her red lipstick being too red or because her curled hair had remained curled, or because things were unfair, it is impossible to say, because you only find out the answers to these things in stories.

But when Emily felt the jolt of the flat of Bernard's work-hardened hand on her, and when she felt her balance failing and her face smack on the brand-new geometric lino she had bought only that week, she knew one thing for certain, Bernard Nacullian was dead meat.

The house remained small after that.

CHAPTER THREE

An Interlude about the City

It's about time I welcomed you to the city.

So, welcome to the city. In this, the first of five interludes, you'll get to know the place the Nacullians call home a little better. In these interludes you'll drive along the city's roads, stroll through its parks, taste the air of the city and even swim in its waters, though the narrator cannot be held responsible for any infectious diseases contracted. In short, I absolutely promise to offer you totally objective and impartial insights into this very real city, because when you know a city, you know its people. So, let's start with the basics, the city-in-the-round, because you've probably never been here, for one.

An important thing to recognise about the city is that no one is 100% sure where it is. By this, I don't mean it's like Atlantis or Tír na nÓg or Utopia, because with those we don't have a clue. Those places are the dandruff of fancy and the sooner we rinse the them out of our imaginations the sooner we can come to see how difficult it is to describe places that actually do exist.

So, while no one is absolutely certain where the city is, the city exists certainly and is in England for certain, in southern England, certainly. But whether it's in the South East or South West is another matter entirely. Most people will tell you it's in the South East, but that's only because those people want to associate themselves with the desultory and debonair metropolitan elites of the capital. Some others will claim it's in the South West, but that's only because they want to see themselves as amiable and honest west-county folk. The truth is that the city is in the middle, but that title's already been taken by the Midlands.

And when I say that the city's in the middle, I'll admit I'm making a fair few assumptions. You see, the good old place is 484 km from Land's End and 309 km from Ramsgate, if you consider Ramsgate as the most easterly point of the south east. Someone might say that makes the city in the south east, for certain. But if you're talking England as a whole, then the most easterly place is Ness Point, which is approximately 684km from the city if you take the coast. Some might say that this makes the city in the south west, certainly. Of course, you needn't take the coast to Ness Point. You could do it as the crow flies or take the M25 and turn off at junction 28. The point I'm making is that these things really aren't that simple, and that's why I'm not absolutely certain where the city is. Though of course I know where it is, because I'm speaking to you from the very same totally objective and impartial city. Hell, I am the city for all you know.

Now, maybe you noticed the city on a weather report and thought, 'I really must go there someday', but you never went there because there was no reason to go there, and there probably won't be any reason to go there after you read this. Though to be fair, there's loads of places like this. Middle places. These islands are fat with middle places, simply suppurating with them. I'm talking about places like Portsmouth or Coventry or

Cwmbran or Bolton or Hull. I'm sorry if that offends anyone from Coventry or Cwmbran or Bolton or Hull, but you get the picture. I'm talking about the places that unless you live there, or your team is playing away, there's hardly any reason to be there. So, you might just be happy enough with seeing the city on the weather report and leave it at that.

Though if you do that, you'd still be making a fair few assumptions, because the city is never simply what you see in a weather report or on a map. The map can show you that the city has its parks and its water and its roads, but abstraction is by its very nature a shallow, flattering thing. See, the city is never simply what some mush sees through misted eyes as he leaves the house for his early morning shift, and neither is the city what someone sees as they jog through midnight streets trying to slough off a cloak of insomnia. The particular is by its very nature a narrow, hard thing, you see. So, the map will not do and your personal experience won't do either. You might ask me what will do then, what will give us the true, objective and totally impartial image of the city? Well, my answer is that I'm not ultimately here for you, am I? I'm here for the Nacullians, who are dotted and smeared about the map of this city as time stumbles on and back and then on again, who exist and who cease to exist and who exist again as we stumble here and there and back again.

But still, as a rule there's little reason to visit the city the Nacullian's call home, even though rules are shallow, flattering things. And of course, there are exceptions to rules, though exceptions are narrow, hard things. Imagine for example you are some Titanic nutcase, by which I mean that you're very fond the RMS Titanic and the lore surrounding it, rather than being vastly sociopathic. If you're a Titanic nutcase, then yes, you'd have good reason to come to the city. And maybe for example you've been doing some Titanic pilgrimage, by which I mean that you've been visiting places associated with the RMS Titanic and the lore surrounding it, rather than roaming to the four corners of the earth in search of God. Well again, yes, you'd have good reason to visit the city.

Because we all know that the Titanic set off from the city on its ill-fated voyage blah blah blah. And so, this Titanic nutcase on her Titanic pilgrimage has just flown over from Belfast after inspecting all things Titanicy in that city where the ill-fated ship was built. And now she's here in this city, likewise investigating all things Titanicy. Maybe her name is Kate or Rose and she's some socialite or writer with too much time on her hands. Anyway, after this city, Kate-or-Rose will be continuing her Titanicy, nutcasey pilgrimage by flying to Cork, another city which was the last stop of the RMS Titanic before the ill-fated ship continued on its ill-fated voyage blah blah blah.

But as we're sailing away from the city itself now, let's take a broader view, because no city is an island and maybe even islands aren't islands after all. Across the water to the south of the city, there's the Isle of Wight, which us city dwellers go to in the summer when we can't stand the boredom anymore. We bob along on the ferry and then drive down to Blackgang Chine for ice-cream or go to Cowes for ice-cream or maybe we don't go at all, but just look out across the water to the island, as we eat our ice-cream. The well-known belief about Wight is that you can fit the entirety of the world's population on the island, but you know, that's got to come with a fair few assumptions. Is everyone supposed to be laying down? Standing up? And if standing, are people allowed to hang out in multi-storey carparks or in the stairwells of large blocks of flats? Are piggybacks allowed? Do children on the shoulders of their parents count? What about people swimming off Shanklin beach? The point I'm making is that these things really aren't that simple.

Then, to the east, there's Pompey. The land of the Skates. Some people here in the city don't have a sufficiently well-developed sense of identity, so they have to hate someone to get a sense of who they aren't, which doesn't necessarily tell them who they are. But that's the case with our abiding hatred of Pompey. Let me illustrate.

I heard a story that once the city council tried to buy an old Second World War flak gun from the ministry of defence. They wanted the gun to bring out and fire in different parts of the city to make things like fetes and car boot sales seem more important and exciting, but the whole plan got scuppered. Somehow, councillors in Pompey heard about the plan and then they wanted their own Second World War flak gun to fire about different parts of their city to make their things seem more important and exciting too.

Things got worse from then on. Requests started coming in for braces of bayonets, then crates of Armalites, half a dozen APCs, batteries of air-to-surface missiles and eventually city councillors were writing to Thatcher asking that she turn significant parts of the UK's nuclear arsenal away from the Soviet Union to target Pompey. Fearing the madness of mutually assured destruction on the south coast, the MoD got skittish and refused all armament demands, so we never got our Second World War flak gun. Though the narrator cannot be held responsible for inaccurate hearsay, it was all because of those Skate cunts and their jealousy.

But that's all in the past, wherever that is. Another interesting thing about the city is that it's also a major destination for Channel Islanders. You know, those people from the Channel Islands who everyone always forgets suffered Nazi invasion and concentration camps. The people of the Channel Islands come over to the city during moonless nights, camouflaged in Higgins boats, or sometimes they fly in by day on budget airlines. They come to the city to drink in chain pubs and shop in chain stores and eat in chain restaurants and everyone assumes they're English. But secretly they're not English, they're Channel Islanders. These Channel Islanders have their own invisible ways and codes and by God they're infiltrating the city without anyone ever knowing about it. They come here because on the Channel Islands there's only beauty and beaches and tax evasion and the remnants of Nazi occupation, whereas in the city there are chain pubs and chain stores and chain restaurants and the cloak of assumed Englishness.

But before we finish I should tell you about something, mush. The term mush will be encountered a number of times and may be unfamiliar to readers, so some advice is in order. Mush is the word we use in this city for people from this city, and if you ever hear it in Pompey then you can be assured that those Skates are just jealous and are copying us. Mush is a deeply meaningful term to the people of this city and it is either a term of familiar endearment or casual indifference or informal hostility, I'm not sure. What I am sure about is how it's pronounced. It's important to note that mush rhymes with push, and if you happen to come to this city not saying mush correctly, you're liable to get a brick in the face.

And that, in overview, is the place you've found yourself in and the place the Nacullians have found themselves in too. A thing that's important to remember in all of this is that the people of this city don't really care about the stuff I've just mentioned, apart from maybe the Pompey stuff and how to get their hands on Second World War artillery. This city might have been the place where the printing press was invented, or the place where the internet was invented, or the place where the Norman invasion landed, or the place where King Cnut held back the waves, but this really doesn't matter to people here, any more than it would to people in Cwmbran or Bolton or Hull. These things are just stories in brochures or on information boards. They're shallow, flattering things. These things don't matter because no one lives the invention of the printing press and no one lives a tide held back by some dead Danish king in an itchy cloak. At least, the Nacullians certainly don't, and that's who I'm concerned with. Yes, I know there's more to the city than the Nacullians, but it's the Nacullians I've chosen, even though they are narrow, hard things.

So, welcome to the city.

CHAPTER FOUR

The Adventures of Thunder the Dog
(1982-1997)

There are too many tales about dogs. This is one of them.

One reason there are too many tales about dogs is that they are very useful for narrators, because they are not really dogs at all, but concentrations of warm and bubbly sentiment. This is why the dog hardly ever gets it in films or books. If the dog ever does get it then you know there's something rotten going on, and by this I mean morally corrupt. Filmmakers will have people beaten and mutilated and shot and have their family businesses asset-stripped by the local fat cat, but Lassie and Benjie and Fido cannot die. They must forever be waiting for their master, even if their master will never come home from sea.

Thunder the dog was a piebald mongrel. Her ancestry was unknown, but if you looked at her lapping up water from the Nacullian's pond or savaging a sycamore twig in the local park, then you would conclude that this mongrel was part Labrador, part Whippet, part Jack Russel and part Mongrel.

She became the Nacullian family dog quite by accident in the autumn of 1982. Inside a concrete pipe that was soon to be plopped into the ground in order to flush shit out into the Itchen river, a small bitch was licking her four cubs, tenderly. This of course was Thunder's mother, who did not have a name, but as far as dogs go, was a good enough mother. Then, a rattling beam of a dodgy flashlight illuminated her.

The dodgy flashlight was Nandad Nacullian's flashlight. When he spotted Thunder's mother he shouted for the crane driver to slack chains and then crawled inside the tube, arms open, and with a there now there now and a shhh shhh, fished the dog and her family out. Thunder's mother grumbled and snapped as Nandad Nacullian crawled towards her, but he knew dogs well enough and when you know dogs, dogs think they know you, the dumb things.

The puppies, still blind and mewing, were handed out to whichever men wanted them, and Thunder's mother was kicked and scrammed off the worksite for her trouble. To be sure, the dog does not get it here, but even kicking and scamming might upset some readers, who will think me morally corrupt. In my defence, I'm simply trying to show you how strongly some people react to fictional worlds where horrible things happen to dogs. This is because dogs are not dogs, but concentrations of warm and bubbly sentiment.

Anyway, it was at random that Nandad picked up a puppy and packed away her small sausagey form in his lunchbox, nestled against some limp lettuce he had removed from his corned beef sandwiches. There was always limp lettuce in his lunchbox, and he resented the fact that no matter how much he complained he didn't like lettuce, Patrice always added it. He never thought that he might make his own bloody sandwiches.

But perhaps enough of sandwiches, because sandwiches are just sandwiches rather than concentrations of warm and bubbly sentiment. When at the end of the day Nandad arrived home with the little whelp in his lunchbox, he was treated as a kind of saviour by the children, because he had brought something new into the house. As Patrice stirred the giant white dumplings in a giant brown stew, she complained that they could not afford another mouth to feed, and there was not only food, but the vet bills too and then there's the dog's business to be dealing with. More and more things and stuff to worry about, she said, though what she secretly meant was that some men do sod-all and get all the credit.

But everyone was ignoring her. Nandad peeled the lettuce off the pup and passed it around his bobbling children. Bernard and Shannon both protested that they would give up a bit of their own food or go without chocolate if they could keep the dog. Even Betty, the eldest, who had been moody of late, emerged from her room to see the new addition to the family. She even smiled and wanted to hold the thing and to know what the dog's name was.

'What'd ye want it to be?' Nandad asked her.

Betty considered this as she stroked the damp little thing. It was possible that she had never been asked to name anything before.

'Thunder.'

Nandad Nacullian squinted and shook his head. 'Funny name for a dog. Why not go for a normal dog's name for Godssake?'

Betty narrowed. 'Ok then. Fido.'

Nandad narrowed his squint. 'Don't get lippy there miss or'll cop you a clip round y'ear. I'm not naming this wee girl dog a wee boy dog's name.'

Betty pulled back from her father's eyes and passed the pup

to Bernard, who had been badgering her for it anyway. Without another word she turned and ran upstairs.

'So, what is her name then Dad?' asked Shannon.

Nandad shrugged: He was getting tired of his children paying him so much attention.

It had been the only real suggestion after all, so he said 'Thunder,' then retreated into the living room and his paper, as he always did before dinner.

About nine months later, Thunder was a dogling who had tripled in size on a diet of old stew, bacon rind and brown bone-shaped biscuits. The novelty had certainly worn off for the family at this point and despite Patrice's insistence that she'd not lift a finger for that dog, feeding Thunder and clearing up her poo and patting her on the head and tossing her bacon rind had tiptoed into the waiting room of habit.

While Thunder didn't mind Patrice feeding her and patting her on the head and tossing her bacon rind, her real devotion was to Nandad. It was a total devotion, in that dumb way so stereotypical of dogs. Her box was next to his worn green armchair, the chair closest to the small colour TV set. After he left for work, Thunder would spend the morning snoozing, surrounded by the smell of him.

To Thunder, and to most dogs, the sensation of smell was something we would not recognise. To call smell smell for a dog, as if it was something similar to our smell, our human sense of smell, is a little like calling a grain of sand West Wittering beach or calling five GCSE grades A* to C real success in life. If a nose could hear, then it would be able to hear a pin drop during a storm and if a nose could see, then it could see the tiny drops of perspiration that gather on the sweaty arms of bricklayers for bluebottles to drink. For the dog, smell is a black touch and a fuzzy music. And it's a smell too. Think reams of smoky colour sliding through some liquid ether, full of direction and song and supple ebbing.

Ah, that's the dog's life. The lucky, dumb things. Thunder could smell a thing and sniff a thing. Thunder's nose was working on the quantum level, it was that sensitive. And to her of course, this amazing thing was like breath or sleep or bacon rind.

Thunder was a lazy dog and a loyal dog who would sleep through the day, but at around 5.15pm would lift herself from her box by the television and make her way to the front door. The rest of the family thought this was some kind of dog magic, dumb bone-fide dog magic. And Thunder was very often right. Nandad would be through the door within half an hour. But the fact was that smells, like lettuce leaves or teeth or anything really, decay. The particular concoction of volatile gasses that made up the signature smell of Nandad Nacullian (black tea, tobacco and Old Spice) was strong in the morning, like a wall. And then brick by brick, the wall would crumble during the day. In Thunder's doggie brain, the wall being at a certain state of disrepair was related in a statistically significant way with Nandad coming home, and this was all.

Of course, Nandad didn't always come home for his faggots and gravy or his gammon and spuds or his stew and dumplings. There were nights when the wall seemed beyond repair and under the mazy yellow of 60-Watt bulbs, she would schlep back to her box. On evenings such as these, Thunder would sense a tiny doom, for dogs can only experience tiny doom, whereas us humans have massive doom, quantum-doom, dog-nose doom. Us unlucky, smart little things.

On nights such as these, Patrice would pace more, smoke more and turn the TV channel over more, in jabbing barks of static. These things were related in a statistically significant way with Thunder's tiny doom and her brown eyes would look up at Patrice, wondering if Patrice would bite her or not.

On evenings such as these, long after the TV had been switched off and the 60-Watt bulbs had gone off and the house was dark, Thunder would smell a knock at the door. Then smell the metal tang of keys and then the metal tang of commercial lager and whiskey. Upstairs, Patrice would pace.

Thunder did not bark.

It was some years later, 1995 in fact, and as Nandad Nacullian had got older, the wall of his volatile gases had tended to remain constant throughout the day. This was known to humans as retirement. Thunder herself had gotten older too, but no matter how old dogs get they never retire. Dogs is dogs is dogs, as they say.

However, to Thunder, while the constancy of Nandad's smell was of comfort, another smell had slowly been scrambling up the wall and plopping down, crepitating and sweaty, into Thunder's sensory garden. It began with a there now there now and a shhh shhh, and at first Thunder paid it no heed. For every dog knows that smells come and smells go and this was the way of the world.

But this smell stayed and slowly it became part of the wall.

And not of Bernard's or Shannon's or Greg's or Patrice's wall, but the wall that was Nandad Nacullian's particular wall. This was a smell half burnt and red raw, a flicksy-flocksy, sharp jabber of a smell, a leather-tough leather-smooth sort of reek, a sugarpaper and sandpaper pong, a dithyrambic and crescendo song, a stink.

Obviously, a dog would never think in these terms, but nevertheless, a translation from doggie-nose-speak into English might be of benefit to the reader. And if anyone who speaks English doesn't yet know what I'm going on about, then I'll spell it out to you. Thunder was smelling a growing and rather malignant cancer hanging about Nandad Nacullian's balls.

Now, dogs know nothing about cancer when compared with your oncologist or your family doctor or even your average dickhead in a Bitterne pub for that matter. But knowing and smelling are two different things and the quantum-nose of the average mutt links the smell of cancer in a statistically significant way with tiny doom. This is an old thing, a deep-old thing, a thing from a part of dogs that they don't need to know about, just be about.

When watching the television amid a fug of ailing fag smoke, Nandad had taken to scratching his balls in discomfort, which unbeknownst to him, sent up another fug of flicksy-flocksy sharp-jabber from his growing and rather malignant cancer. Thunder sneezed and felt tiny doom and then fell back to a restless slumber under the TV's cackle and fizz. On the TV was a tuxedoed and flabby comedian who was addressing a live audience in the Albert Hall. In one hand he held a pink sausage-shaped balloon and was feigning incompetence at making a balloon animal. This was very funny to the audience in the Albert Hall because they knew from the comedian's own reputation that he was in fact very good at making balloon animals. As he struggled and fumbled further so the mirth of the Albert Hall grew, until Nandad could stand it no longer and switched to BBC1. Anyway, the comedian is dead now and no-one in the twenty-first century remembers him or would find him funny.

It was one afternoon soon after this that Patrice and Nandad came through the door barking and whining at one another, which in English meant they were shouting and crying. On the chequered lino of the kitchen floor Thunder had left a long puddle of green piss, which was testament to the fact that everyone had been out longer than usual, and that Thunder's bladder wasn't what it used to be.

After being kicked and scrammed into the garden Thunder cheered herself up by mauling a sycamore twig and drinking from the little slab-lined pond. The dull day grew duller and still the back door did not open to let her in. It began to rain and as the droplets made the pond's surface quiver and spit, Thunder tried to hide under the privet hedge that separated the Nacullians' from the Clemenses' next door. She felt tiny doom, poor thing, and it was not until well after the dull day had become dark that yellow 60-Watt bulbs suddenly burst on throughout the house and the back door opened.

In the days and weeks after this the flicksy-flocksy smell had started to become something of its own entirely, like a new member of the household. What had once been an addition to Nandad Nacullian's smell wall was now something apart from him, but always near him. It was sat next to him as he watched the telly, it stalked him about the house and into the garden shed, where he would hammer and nail at half-finished birdboxes. It would steal scraps from his dinnerplate and would maul at his hand as he buckled over from ever more frequent agonies. And Thunder's pack instinct, her noble and dumb and deep pack instinct, was set off by all this into a flurry of tiny doom. And who could blame her, for it was like a snake in the den, a foreign dog on the horizon. It had to either be avoided or attacked, but could be neither.

The Nacullians were at the dinner table and it was hot-brown-salty-wet globlets time, which is known to humans as Sunday roast. Thunder had learned a long time ago that she was the last of the pack to benefit from hot-brown-salty-wet globlets time and that if she begged or whined or attempted to get a share she would be kicked and scrammed to a time and place without hot-brown-salty-wet globlets. And so, she gazed up at her pack and bided her time on the chequered kitchen lino.

At the fold-out dinner table three generations of Nacullian were yapping and growling as much as usual, when Nandad put down his loaded fork and stared ahead. Thunder noticed this immediately because her doggie brain thought it possible she'd get thrown a really big hot-brown-salty-wet globlet. Then, slowly, the rest of the family stopped their growling and seemed to focus on Nandad, who had begun, quiet at first, to whine. The whine built and soon became the kind of whine that gave Thunder the sense of an old thing, a deep-old thing, a thing from a part of dogs that they don't need to know about, just be about. It was a mortal whine of sharp-jabber and smoky ether. It was the thing apart from her master, but near her master.

Thunder felt a growl bubble in her throat. Nandad swung his

legs around his chair and pulled himself up to standing. The family looked at him and barked and started to whine.

Then Thunder saw it. The snake in the den. The fire sweeping the across the plains. The snarling lips of a foreign dog. Not near her master. But on her master. A totalising tiny doom. And Thunder could not control herself.

So she snapped at the thing, the dark thing, which by unhappy coincidence looked to everyone else like she was attacking Nandad's balls. It looked like this to Nandad too, who fell back against the kitchen table shouting, 'Woah! You feckin' crazy she-bitch!' and he kicked out at Thunder, his tartan slipper scraping the end of her nose. Now, if you've ever been hurt in the balls or been a dog that's been hurt in the nose, you might imagine that these experiences are equally painful and unpleasant, but if you've never been a dog or never been hurt in the balls then I'm sure you won't know what I'm talking about. And if you're a dog that's been hurt in the nose and in the balls, then you've my sympathy.

But anyway, at this seeming attack, the family was on its feet and Nandad was on the floor. The kitchen was awash with whining and barking and snarling. Thunder experienced a world of kicking and scramming and rain and shiver that night, but even under the privet hedge next to the fence, she could still smell the fug of the foreign dog which was somehow still inside, mauling her master.

It was a kind of dog magic, the family said after. A dumb bone-fide kind of dog magic. Thunder had known all along and we were too late, they said, too late to save him. We should have listened to her. We should have heeded her. Good dog, they said. Loyal dog, they said.

Things then improved for Thunder. Patrice even apologised by letting her on her lap while she watched Last of the Summer Wine on Sunday afternoons. Thunder's hot-brown-salty globlets share was increased and her failing bladder was looked on with more sympathy and less kick-and-scram.

And around the house, the sharp-jabber smell of foreign dog fell away, quiet and quick. But more slowly, the wall of Nandad's volatile gases crumbled and collapsed, until there was nothing but a faint quantum whiff of it. In doggy-nose-speak this meant he had died, and in English this meant the same also.

So, in this story the dog did not get it at all and so I'm not morally corrupt. Thunder just missed her master. Yes, there are too many tales about dogs. This was one of them.

CHAPTER FIVE

Fryer
(1990)

James Radley was sat in the far corner of The Garden Wall, a cold pint of cider in one hand and a freshly lit fag in the other. To an onlooker at the main bar the man would have looked distant and contemplative, almost serene in fact, but the truth was that James Radley was bursting, and I don't mean for a piss. James Radley was pyroclastic-volcano-bursting, shook-up-bottle-of-pop bursting, know-the-answer-to-the-million-dollar-question bursting.

Two things had recently happened in James' life which he was simply dying to speak about, but was unable to speak about. Now, there are many reasons we are unable to speak about things, but the most pressing reason James couldn't speak about these things was that his wife, Emily, was about to show up. She had rung the pub fifteen minutes before and James had seen as the barman picked up the receiver of the nicotine beige BT Viscount 9631AR Super 4 telephone and nodded toward him. 'Yes', he saw the barman's lips say, 'Yes, he's here.' Then, 'It's the Mrs, James. Wants to know if she should come down for a drink.'

About half the bar turned toward him to await his answer.

Suddenly, James could hear the low mumble of the sports commentary from the TV at the end of the bar. Of course he didn't want her here. Of course he didn't want her here disturbing his fraught contemplation, disturbing his bursting, but what could he say? If she had asked him before he left for work this morning, in the privacy of their kitchen, then he could have just told her to leave off, or told her that he was working late. But now she had ambushed him, the bitch, and people were staring at him, seeing if he was going to tell his Mrs to piss off or if he was going to cave and let her come down.

'Fine by me,' he shrugged.

The barman lipped this news down the phone, then replaced the yellowy receiver. The bar returned to the sports commentary and James returned to controlling the shook-up bottle of pop that was his psyche.

Mr James Radley was the proprietor of Chippy Chips, the best and only provider of chippy chips and related foods on the Harefield estate. It was true that the Chinese place three shops down did serve chips, but they weren't chippy chips and they had been relegated on the menu to their 'English Dishes' section, as one of four possible options: chips, omelette, chicken omelette and chips in oyster sauce. No, Wok on the Wild Side wasn't a threat to James Radley.

Sometimes the proprietor of Chippy Chips would have a laugh and call the place three doors down Chinky Chips, because you see, chippy sounds a little bit like chinky and the people three doors down were chinky, whereas James wasn't chinky, but he did run a place with 'chippy' in the name, and that's what made the joke funny.

But seriously though, he didn't mind the Chinese lot three

doors down, Anna and Alan and their son Andy and that little girl of theirs, Alice. They were alright, just as long as they didn't start to sell chippy chips and battered haddock, because then he'd be forced to tear up their whole slitty-eyed operation, crumble the whole fortune-cookie, burn down the entire fucking pagoda. But, you know, they were alright.

But anyway, James was bursting, like I said, and now he had finished half of his cider and was stubbing out his fag in a glassy green ashtray. Then his wife walks in. Emily. The barman nods to her and she starts to scan the room. And she sees him. Her James. Her hubby James. And she starts to walk over. She's tarted up, is Emily, with her red lipstick and her hair in curls and she's in her heels and her thin little lady-cigarette is in her mouth. And James is bursting.

'You buying me a drink then, wonderboat?' says Emily.

James puts his hand in his jean's pocket and pulls out a crumpled fiver.

'Whatever you want love, and I'll have another one of these.' He downs the rest of his cider.

While Emily is walking to the bar and James is sat there still bursting, I've enough time to tell you what he's bursting about.

The first thing he was bursting to talk about was his new fryer, or frying range as it was called in the frying business. This frying range was called a frying range because this thing was not just a fryer but a whole new real deal that would transform James Radley's own personal frying business. It had two chip pans, three top boxes, a fish pan, scrap box, and on the far left, one more fish pan and one more chip pan. Auto filtering, automatic temperature control. All new. All gleaming. No warranty, no manual, but no questions asked and a 50% discount with free delivery. He might even move into Thornhill with the old frying range and set up another Chippy Chips. Yes, this was going to change James' frying business.

James was really pleased with his frying range, but he was aware that people weren't in general that interested in talking about frying ranges. Sometimes, James wished there was another chippy on the estate so he'd have someone to talk to about oil ratios, and prep-time and how long you can keep a piece of skate under the heat lamp before it'll make someone sick. But then he remembered Alan. Chinese Alan, three doors down who ran Wok on the Wild Side. He made chips too. He fried things and he made chips. Oh, not chippy chips, not proper English food, but maybe Alan would like a conversation, would like to come over one afternoon, take a Wok on the Wild Side and visit Chippy Chips with its brand-new frying range.

Emily was back with a pint of cider and small glass of red. She popped herself down on a stool across from James and finished her lady-cigarette with one long drag. James looked at her quizzically, because he didn't expect her back so quickly and in fact, neither did I. So, it turns out I didn't have time to tell you about the second thing James Radley was bursting about after all. Sorry about that. But Emily is bound to go to the toilet at some point, so I promise to tell you then.

'Aren't you going to tell me I look nice?' asked Emily as she stubbed her cigarette out.

'Ok. You look nice. Aren't you going to say thanks for the drink?'

'Fine. Thanks for the drink.' She took a glug of her wine.

'What brings you down here then?'

'It's Friday. Friday brings me down here. It's not unusual for someone to have a drink with her husband on a Friday night, you know?'

'But what about the kids?'

'Oh, I turned the gas on and left 'em with a box of matches to play with.'

'Just a bloody question, woman.'

Emily sighed, 'Andy's looking after them.'

'Who the hell's Andy then? And why's he looking after my kids?'

'God, you know who Andy is. Andy. Alan's son, Andy. Andy Pho. He's so good with kids. Jimmy and Jade love him.'

'You left the kids with him?'

'Yeah. Gave him a few quid and told him there's some chicken omelette left over in the fridge. He babysat for us New Year's Eve last year!'

James sipped meditatively at his pint. 'Did he?'

Emily didn't bother responding. She flipped open her packet of thin lady-cigarettes and popped one in her gob. Then she leant over toward her husband.

'Would you mind?' she asked, as she wagged her finger at her lady-cigarette.

'Haven't you got a lighter?'

'Yeah but...Christ, there's no such thing as gentlemanly behaviour anymore, is there?'

'What do you mean? I just bought you a drink!'

'Which I went to the bar for!'

Emily leant back and searched around in her denim jacket pocket for her own lighter. God, James was really bursting now. And because it doesn't look like Emily will be going for a piss anytime soon I may as well jump in and tell you the second thing

James Radley was bursting to talk about, but couldn't talk about.

The other thing he was bursting to talk about was the fact that he had impregnated Shannon Nacullian when she was fifteen years old, and today, he had seen his son for the first time in years. He knew more about frying ranges than he did human biology, but still, he felt he really needed to talk to someone about the mechanics and nitty-grittys of what had taken place back in 1985.

But he couldn't. He couldn't because firstly his wife was sat in front of him and second, because he didn't trust anyone enough not to tell his wife. He also felt that some people might take exception to him impregnating a fifteen-year-old, not that pregnant fifteen-year-olds weren't common enough throughout the east of the city. However, pregnant fifteen-year-olds made pregnant by married men in their thirties with two kids, were.

So, all this suppurating stuff about the new fryer and Shannon Nacullian had to be held down, held back. And here was Emily getting into one of her moods about the death of gentlemanly behaviour because she had to light her own fag. And soon it would be that men-are-pigs stuff, all that whinging, whining men-are-pigs stuff.

'You know, some men James, are just pigs. They're real bloody pigs.'

From the end of the bar there was a ragged cheer. Someone had just scored something in some sport. With his eyes fixed on Emily, James was nodding, his arms folded. He had heard about Shannon giving birth back in the day, and remembered folks wondering about who the father was. Another kid from school, most likely. Some guy from the other side of the city, probably. When one of James' mates joked that he'd not have minded being the dad if he got to give one to that Shannon Nacullian, James laughed the loudest. Maybe too loud, he worried afterwards.

It had started innocently enough when James offered Shannon free chips if she flashed her knickers. Shannon had come into the shop one night, half-cut and giggling with a friend. She ordered a small chips with salt and vinegar and James told her there'd be a five-minute wait. Shannon's friend was way more gone than she was and soon tottered outside to vomit by Wok on the Wild Side. Shannon was wearing a black mini skirt and a tied-up denim shirt. They were alone, and James thought it would be a laugh, so he asked her.

He remembered they were white, with little red flowers on.

After that it was a free battered sausage if she'd flash her tits and the rest was pretty much inevitable. James remembered Shannon's pale piggy eyes as he fucked her on a cushioned crate of spuds out the back. She had looked uncomfortable, but then all the women James Radley had ever fucked had looked uncomfortable, so the man wasn't to know really.

For a while after that James became worried that he was being exploited, because Shannon was coming in almost daily for her free chips and sausage with curry sauce and walking away without so much as a handjob. It was only when three months later she started to show that he made damn well sure to start charging her. After that her appearances at Chippy Chips, and across the estate for that matter, quickly diminished.

He first saw the sprog about a year later, as she pushed it in a navy and cream 60s pram. Her Mum was with her, and they were passing the shops up toward the doctor's surgery. Chippy Chips was open for the lunch custom and Shannon rushed past, not looking in, her mother rigid beside her. He couldn't see inside the pram, but a little white arm popped up.

The next time was a few months later, as he was mending a fence for old Mrs Curtain. He heard a squeak behind him and then a clatter of quick steps and turned around to see the squished-up mid-scream face of her baby. What a weird little piggy-eyed Nacullian, he thought, and turned back to the job at hand. It would have been poetically appropriate if he had smashed his hand with the hammer at this point, but he didn't, and you can't expect such things to happen in a novel like this.

And finally he had seen them both today for the first time in years. They were walking through the forested cutway by Thornhill Park Road. He could see them coming towards him from a way off and there were no turnings, just the trees and the dirt, so the rest was inevitable. He had smiled to himself initially as he noted from a distance how Shannon had put on weight and how she looked tired holding her grom's hand as he tottered along. The kid was about four now, three or four and, yes, definitely had those same pale piggy eyes he remembered when he fucked Shannon in the chip shop. The kid was dressed in a pair of denim dungarees and was sucking at a large crisp shaped like an animal paw.

A few more steps, and then they were within each other's orbit. But she looked, he didn't know, not like she had before. She'd not looked scared, not nervous, not even pissed off, but passive, totally relaxed, like she didn't know him and he didn't matter.

'Cute little fella,' he found himself saying.

'Name's Greg,' was the reply as she passed. Flat. Neutral. Like he didn't matter.

Like he was a fattening, aging man who owned a chip shop

and wanted to talk about frying ranges that no one else cared about. James couldn't help but turn around, to try and make eye contact, even with the boy. But all he got were their backs as they walked on.

James had looked down then at the uneven concrete path. This was when he started to feel the bursting, and for the first time he said to himself, 'That's mine,' by which he meant the boy, he meant Greg was his. Though the boy wasn't his at all, because how can a teaspoonful of spunk make something yours? Some people have the most insane fucking ideas.

So those are the reasons James Radley was bursting and those are the reasons James Radley could do nothing about the fact he was bursting. Emily was getting impatient too but had found her lighter and had lit her lady-cigarette.

'So, we gonna get drunk and have a good time or are you gonna sit there like a retard all night?' she said.

'Ben!' shouted James all of a sudden. The bar turned to look at him and Emily skew-eyed her hubby wonderboat. 'Ben mush!'

The barman peeled himself away from the TV and walked wearily along the bar.

'What?' said Ben.

'Champagne Ben. I want a bottle of champagne!'

'You celebrating something then?'

'Yeah, are we celebrating something then?' said Emily.

Yes, thought James, yes I am celebrating. I'm celebrating my new frying range with its auto-filtering and automatic temperature control and the 50% discount with free delivery. I'm celebrating my son, who's three or four now and has piggy-pale Nacullian eyes. I'm celebrating the fact I fucked Shannon Nacullian on top of a box of Crown Royal Maris Piper spuds. Yes,

I'm fucking celebrating.

James looked at his wife.

'Nothing special,' he replied to no one in particular.

'Well,' said Ben the Barman, 'we don't have any champagne.' He looked round down by his feet for a moment before pronouncing, 'We got Prosecco and Blue Nun is all.'

Hubby wonderboat looked at Emily, eyebrows raised.

'Give us a bottle of the Dirty Nun then,' called Emily, 'But you're going to the bloody bar this time James.'

Seven minutes later, James Radley's face was looking like a crushed fag packet. He pulled the half-empty wine glass away from his lips. 'This,' he said, 'This is shit. Like drinking perfume.' He mulled some words on his palate, 'Like cold perfume.'

Emily was on to her second glass. 'I think it's lovely. Like drinking perfume.' She mulled some words on her palate, 'Like cold perfume,' and she downed half her glass, before giving a burp and a chuckle. 'Careful there, Em,' she warned.

The Garden Wall was starting to fill up with the Friday night crowd. The older lot were ordering steaks and scampi and pies and settling into corners with their other halves. The younger ones were stood around the bar with bottles of foreign larger and pints of English lager and glasses of wine that tasted like cold perfume. They would be having a few at The Garden Wall before heading into town. Avenues of love and vomit and late-night chips in Bevois Valley were opening up in the timeline of the universe.

James was sipping at another pint of cider as he stared at the blemishless cream legs of a girl he knew must be underage.

He saw a hand, a man's hand, come across to rest on her small sequined arse.

'James?'

'Yeah?'

'You're not looking at me, James.'

'Just thinking.'

James was thinking how he'd like to be that hand resting on the sequined arse.

'Haven't you got something to tell me James?'

James blinked. He looked at his wife. He thought. It couldn't be, he thought. Any conversation about the Kinomile 4000x frying range would have been lost on her.

'No. Don't think so.'

'You're such a fucking pig.' There was a chuckle in Emily's throat and she was shaking her head.

James scanned the now crowded and noisy room. No one was looking at them. 'I'm a pig, eh? How's that then?'

Emily gave a flappy sigh. 'Happy 40th,' she cooed across the table. 'I suppose this must turn you from a pervert into an old pervert.'

'You remembered then.' Flat. Neutral. Another sip of cider.

'Come on, I wouldn't forget hubby wonderboat's birthday now, would I? Wouldn't miss the chance to remind him how much older he is than me now, would I?' Here Emily winked, and James thought she must have thought it was a sexy wink.

Emily happily swished back her wine, took a deep breath of fuggy pub air, and then reached under the table. A moment later she lifted up an oblong box wrapped in newsprint and placed it in front of James.

'So, happy birthday, wonderboat.' She pointed to the box.

'See? I made it look like a chip box. With the newspaper and everything.'

'Very creative.' Flat. Neutral. Another sip of cider.

'Now, I've put a lot of thought into this James, so if you don't like it you've got to promise to lie to me. Right?'

'Right,' said James, 'I promise I'll lie to you.'

James reached for the box.

'Don't lift it up!' said Emily.

He stilled his hand over it. 'Why not?'

'Might give away what it is.'

'Em, opening it up will give away what it is.'

'Oh come on Jamesey. Just play along.'

'Well what am I meant to do then?'

'Just, just open it without lifting it up.'

James sighed and started to tear at the newsprint on top of the box. Probably a joke, he thought. Probably a box of wooden forks or a frying range catalogue or a jar of pickled eggs. Shit, it could even be a fish supper.

It was a brown cardboard box, like a shoebox.

Emily was smiling madly now, nervously now. 'Go on. Open it then. It's not a pair of shoes if that's what you're thinking.'

James pushed in the little clip at the side and flicked it out. Then he flipped the lid up and over. In the middle, cellotaped to the centre of the base of the box, was a stick. A white stick. A white plastic stick.

'What the 'ells this?'

Emily skew-eyed her hubby wonderboat and said nothing.

James slowly tore the tape to release the stick. He picked up the white plastic stick and examined it. At one end of the plastic white stick there was a coloured band. The coloured band at the end of the white plastic stick was blue.

'You happy James?' said Emily.

A pause. A white pause. 'Yeah. Yeah I'm happy.'

'You're not lying to me, now James? James, you really are happy, aren't you, James?'

CHAPTER SIX

Pass
(1984)

Her mother keened and she would not stop. In the white room. By the window. In the warm room. By the bed. To the ears of her two other children it had begun as a kind of sigh, a low and tremulous spastic sigh, but it had built, and it would not stop. The sound slid up to their gullets and then crawled down, spiked and sallow, into their stomachs. It was an old thing, a deep-old thing, a thing from a part of them that they didn't want to know about. It was an alien thing, a cold, black, coal-black alien thing, a thing from a part of themselves they did not know. A thing of grief, urgent and formal.

The thin curtains around the bed were drawn, but her children, standing around their sister, their unconscious sister, fading sister, were deeply aware of the ward around them. They knew that others lay beyond other blue curtains. They knew that those others were listening to the deep-old thing that invaded the air from the open mouth of their mother. As their mother continued, the hands of the other daughter, Shannon, reached out to stop her, but they would not stop her, and Shannon's hands fell back to her side. In the blank blue which wrapped them into this room without walls, the children could not focus on their sister, nor their mother, nor on each other. And so, they stared blankly at a sign above the bed, where in chalk a name was written: Betty Nacullian.

So, these Nacullians were standing around the bed with the mother keening and the children wishing this would be over, all over. And it soon would be over. Soon after this, they were all taken into a side room of files and narrow chairs and told the news, the news not new, which they already knew, that Betty was not coming back from this one. The poor girl was not coming back from this one, the poor girl, her mother said. She was not crying and would not cry, not even at the funeral, which the children thought strange, for even their father had cried, and he had not even bothered to come to the hospital this time, this last time before it was all over. Maybe he knew their mother would embarrass them with her deep-old coal-black thing, they wondered. But why couldn't she just have cried?

'Is she comfortable?' Patrice asked the calm eyes of the Sister, who was sitting across the narrow table.

'Yes,' said the Sister. 'Yes, she is. As far as anyone can know.'

'Ah yes,' said Patrice, who nodded and then bent slightly forwards.

Stood behind her, Shannon and Bernard knew something was changing in their mother. A giving out or giving in or giving way or giving up was under way. The Sister had reached over to Patrice across the laminate table and had covered their mother's hand with her own big, well-oiled hand. Her calm eyes were looking into their mother's face, a face they could not see, and they thought their mother was crying, that maybe she was crying now? But she was not crying, she later told her children, and she

47

would not cry. Not even at the funeral.

So, they stood there, and their mother sat there and the Sister sat there, facing them. And faint faint, and small small, they both began to feel hungry. Yes, it was true that their sister Betty was about to die but the fact was that it was now two o'clock, and they usually had lunch at noon.

Before she was dead, Betty was the eldest child, at least that's how everyone saw her. Today, no one really talks about Betty Nacullian. Not because she has been forgotten, but because no one really ever understood what had happened to her, and so talking can seem useless.

Betty was an exceptionally pale child and for a white family who were themselves on the pale side, she was known as the pale one and was often called the pale one in that way which is half affection and half criticism. Patrice though was concerned by this paleness and worried it signalled a sickliness or a case of malnutrition, so she always tried to stuff her daughter with good things like beef and eggs and full fat milk and dripping and tea. To any outside observer it was clear early on that this made not a bit of difference to the paleness of the pale one. Patrice though persevered and by the age of seven, Betty was a chubby little thing, a chubby little thing who was as pale as she had ever been.

Once when she was eight, Nandad took her on a daytrip to West Wittering beach and forgot the sunblock. No one remembers why he didn't take the younger kids, but the material point was that two hours later she was on her way to the hospital, crimson and raw and screaming on the hot leatherette seats of Nandad's Vauxhall Velox. Patrice did not speak to him for a month after that and took permanent revenge by putting lettuce in his sandwiches forever after. Weeks later when Betty's burns had healed she simply slipped right back to her former paleness and avoided all trips to the beach thereafter.

Betty had first attempted suicide at the age of thirteen when she pushed herself into the road as an ice-cream van came jingling around the corner. The van braked just in time, with Paul Dunkford the ice-cream man screaming at her as he shook uncontrollably. Grazed only, Betty picked herself up off the road and quietly apologised before ordering cider lollies, one for herself, Shannon and Bernard.

This was the first, but these attempts formed a cycle, around once every nine months, like a birth. Betty's fourth birth was the last. If you had asked her what her life was like that would make her want to do such things she wouldn't have understood the question, for the question presumes we all have a life to be like this or like that with. Betty didn't consider this so, and when people said things like, 'my life is going nowhere', 'life's down the shitter at present', 'life has been turned upside-down' or 'Fuck. Life, eh?', she didn't know what they meant, and this made her feel all the worse.

Betty had no life, but she did have an existence, and this she was clear was the existence she was working to end. From day to day since the first attempt, her mind was a picture show of possible ways and means. With a rope, with a razor, with pills, in the road, in the woods, with bleach, on the common, in the park, in a carpark, with glass, with milk bottle glass, with a jump, with a failed jump, in a pact, in her room, in protest, in a cry for help, by sheer accident, by sheer need, in a back room laden with gloom, in a churchyard laden with gloom, fairground laden with gloom, in a rec-ground laden with home, laden with him, laden with her, with them.

The second time she used a bicycle innertube. When he had found her in his shed Nandad Nacullian's first thought was that he had finally gotten to the bottom of where that blasted innertube had gone to. At this point still, the family thought all this death business was a phase, or a blip or just one of those things, and would pass. To try and cheer her up Nandad made a bird table for the back garden with some wood he had pilfered from work. He had initially intended it to be a dog kennel for Thunder, but daughters were more important than dogs, he said to her, and he knew she liked watching the sparrows.

The bird table was built, but it happened again all the same, intolerable and inevitable. And the family, in their own ways tiny tiny, and in their own ways slow slow, were moving towards accepting that maybe she had to die, or would simply die, eventually. Their efforts to keep her alive, to protect her from herself, to build her bird houses and bring her pets, to keep her away from pills, from razors, away from the road, away from the woods, away from glass, from milk bottle glass, away from places laden with gloom, laden with them, all waned. Slowly, like nails growing or like hair growing, they all realised that Betty's existence really was her own, in the smallest and most eventual of ways, yes, it was hers, and her family could not keep her away from her own existence.

And so quietly they left her to herself, to be herself or not be herself. By the age of fifteen, Betty had become something of a writer, or that's how Patrice sometimes described her, 'something of a writer', in that way which is half affection, half criticism.

Betty would fill up diaries and pads and notebooks with anything from autobiography, meteorological comments, shopping lists, haiku and pictures of stick men and stick women and stick dogs that you'd need a psychoanalyst to tell you the meaning of. Apart from Patrice's vague ambivalence to her daughter's scrawling, no-one in the family paid any attention to the small column of notepads that grew from the side of her bed.

It was only later, a few months after her death, that anyone went near Betty's little cairn of words. One day as Patrice was manically and mechanically cataloguing her daughter's things, she slowed down and opened up a pad and began to review and preview the books and notebooks and diaries her daughter had filled up. Over the next couple of weeks, Patrice found many things.

Things like:

21st October
The century is closing now. It's only 1983 but I'm feeling it start to close. There are songs about it on the radio. Children in schools draw pictures of it, and everyone is hovering in the air, smiling. Films pretend they know what the twenty-first century will be like, and all the cars gravitate in the air, shining. The kids copy this and draw their pictures. Yes, soon it will be closed and I have to close myself before it closes itself. If I can't close myself and the new century comes, the terrible century, the century of the falling of everything, like Nostradamus said, like the IMF says, like Faiz says. If I can't close myself and I end up dying in 2040, I don't know how I'll live with it.

Patrice, deeply affected though she was, did not know what

to make of this, but knew for certain that it must have had something to do with that coloured fella.

That coloured fella was Betty's boyfriend, Faiz. He was a sweet and complicated boy from Shirley, over on the other side of the city. They had met one day in town as they were waiting in line at Wimpy.

'What're you ordering?' he asked her.

'Burger and fries,' replied Betty.

'Same here,' said Faiz, and it was love.

They might only have started off with burgers and fries in common, but this grew. Faiz liked folk music and the age of steam and while Betty could think of nothing more pointless than folk music and steam power, she humoured him, because that's what she thought you had to do with a man. Once, she went with him on a date to see some guy called Martin Carthy in a tiny club in Portswood. It was dark in there and there were candles in jam jars and everyone was sat down. As well as the old singer with his old guitar there was an old guy with a violin too, which Faiz later told her was a fiddle. The only thing she had liked about it all was the darkness, which had hidden her embarrassment, as well as their tightly enfolded hands.

She had even tolerated a steam-powered date from New Alresford to Alton on the Watercress Line, which Faiz had got as a surprise for their two-month anniversary. She had smiled the whole time and had nodded as Faiz discussed the wonders of standard gauge tracks and the comforts of more innocent times.

Betty took Faiz's virginity casually, one evening under a bush in Palmerston Park. She did this because she knew how and because she knew that no one else would. Unlike most boys, Faiz didn't move on after this, a notch on the stick, but clung to her because he knew how and because he knew no one else would.

He told her his secrets too. These began with things like the secret of how he cheated on his art coursework by submitting a photocopy of something by Andy Warhol. The art teacher thought this was some kind of a statement and gave him an A, though Faiz had always felt bad about it. Then there was the secret about how he left his cousin having a fit in the middle of the street because he was scared and didn't know what to do. Then a little later came the secret of how his father beat him and the secret of how the beating came from love, came because his father did not know what else to do with him, because Faiz was soft, because there's no way Faiz could command a woman, a life, a family, a future.

And Patrice was right in a way, it was Faiz who convinced Betty that the whole twenty-first century idea was a bad thing from the off. It was him who wedded the theories of Nostradamus to IMF long-term forecasts cut from his father's spent copies of the Financial Times. All this was married with vague suspicions that there was no way the future could be as good as the past, that somehow the future was dying. Not stopped exactly, but dying, moribund.

And Fiaz told Betty to look. The IRA bombing campaign was now well into its second decade, and look, they had bombed the city not so long ago and had nearly taken out Maggie Thatcher in Brighton, what else were they going to do? And look, there was famine in Ethiopia and then LiveAid comes along, and look, all these musicians are singing about starving people who don't know it's Christmas, and the super-rich are asking the poor to give them money to stop the famine. What were these musicians going to do next? Then there was the fact that the East threatened nuclear apocalypse and the West threatened nuclear apocalypse. Was that going to work out well? They were in a world of primed nuclear weapons, highly effective terrorists and insincere musicians with horrible hair. You really think we're on course to do well in the next century, Betty?

No, thought Betty, no. No, it was not going to work out well and though Faiz seemed wild at times, she didn't think that a teenager who wept after sex and loved folk music and travelling from New Alresford to Alton on the Watercress Line could be that wild. Yes, Betty was, yes, slowly becoming convinced. Nostradamus and the IMF. The IRA and LiveAid. Yes, it all made sense, and Faiz had not even touched on the Holocaust or the Bengal famine or Cliff Richard's latest album. Of course, all these horrors were a given, weren't they, they were the background to the world being the world, but it was the things like LiveAid that really tipped the thing over the edge and meant there was no hope whatsoever.

If Betty had been honest about it though, all of Faiz's conspiracy and hopelessness talk was for her just a way of making an unshakeable intuition credible. This was the intuition, the simple certainty, that nothing was ever going to get better. For Betty, the IRA and the IMF and LiveAid and Nostradamus were just the clothes which covered a naked faith.

But she nodded at Faiz as these new ideas dried and hardened into the shape of her intuition. And soon she did not just listen to him, but she began to chip in, then sometimes even take the lead, to tell Faiz about the coming time, about the burning-out of history. Then teeny teeny and ickle ickle, change came. As Betty's belief in Faiz's theories increased, she noticed that Faiz was starting to draw back, starting to mollify his predictions of disaster. The burning-out of history became more of a sunburn and the coming certainties became vague possibilities.

Things became worse for Betty when she noticed that sometimes Faiz even sounded hopeful. He started to say things like, 'you'll be ok', 'how about a weekend in Bognor?', 'I saw something quite interesting on ITV last night' and 'Betty, I love you.' This hypocrisy in him was galling, was intolerable, but, reflected Betty, it was inevitable. Because nothing was ever going to get better, was it?

Soon after that, Betty gave birth for the third time. And this time, there was blood. When he found out, Faiz had rushed to the hospital with his brown eyes beating and his bottom lip pursing, but he was stopped outside the ward by the long arms and firm eyes of Patrice Nacullian. He tried to reason with her, to tell her how much he loved and how much he cared, but there was no way he could see her again. It was a family decision Patrice told him, and Faiz knew that families are impossible to ignore, whatever we think of them.

Back in the side room of files and narrow chairs, Patrice straightened herself and withdrew her hand from across the laminate table. She stood up and told the Sister she'd have to take the kids for a bit of lunch, as it was after two o'clock, and they usually had lunch at noon. She'd be back though, she said, and would spend the night with Betty, she said.

After their lunch in the hospital canteen, Shannon and Bernard were sent home on the bus, with strict instructions on how to mash potatoes and cook faggots and scrape up dog poo and restock the bird table for the sparrows. They were not to expect their father home that night and if he did come home, they were to stay in their rooms.

On the bus back they sat on the top deck at the front, and stared out at the long, limp, endless string that was Shirley High Street. Shannon was quiet as they rumbled along, but Bernard began to complain. Betty could have been ok, he claimed, if only she had managed to pull herself together and had manned up and had taken it on the chin and had got over herself and had put first things first. If she had done all these things, he assured himself and Shannon, she would have been fine. Because what's the problem, he spat towards his sister, what's the problem with normal life? Perhaps Betty was scared of something that wouldn't happen, or perhaps she thought she was too la-de-da for normal, regular life. Shannon just stared out of the front of the lurching bus and said nothing, because she thought there was nothing to say.

Patrice came home early the next morning as Shannon and Bernard's spoons waded through bowls of half-cooked porridge. They looked to one another when they heard the tinkle of keys in the front door but did not move. When their mother walked into the kitchen, she immediately spotted the deficiently-cooked porridge and told Shannon so, adding that their sister was gone now, and they'd have to ask their teachers for Friday off so as to go to the funeral.

And creak creak and stumble stumble, Friday came. To the family's surprise, the service at St Mochta's was a middling-large one, as numbers had been swelled by relatives from over the water and by people around the estate who had recently realised they knew Betty very well and needed to pay their respects. The weather that day was a kind of nothing, neither still nor breezy, overcast or clear, hot or cold. It left the people who gathered outside after with little to say by way of small talk, and so people were only left to tut, smoke, and then leave.

Inside St Mochta's during the service, Bernard and Shannon had made quiet and certain vows to themselves, because that's what you do when people die. It's the old, I'll-always-something-this and the classic, I'll-never-something-that, but it's always something somewhere in the middle, and it never lasts. Shannon stood silent as the priest raised his arms up and down and she promised herself, in herself, that her first child would be called Betty and she promised herself, in herself, that of course her first child would be a girl.

And for Bernard, as he gazed upon a stained-glass man giving another stained-glass man a set of stained-glass keys, he promised himself he would never cry again and would instead make rollups or casually pick his nose as an appropriate substitute. It turned out he couldn't keep this promise, for who could, but when he grew up he did pick his nose and smoke a lot of rollups.

The wake came after. For family only, it was held in Thornhill working men's club. Back in the late 60s around the time Betty was born, Nandad had helped build the place and had stayed friendly with the secretary, Glen Kostek. Glen had been one of the tutters and smokers and leavers after the funeral and he had pulled some strings to give the family half-price hire of the bar area, plus free cocktail sausages and twiglets.

It was mid-afternoon and the wake was slumbering on.

Bernard and Shannon were sitting in their corner of the saloon with their lemonades and cheese and onion crisps. Across the room, their parents' relatives had formed an enclosure around the principal mourners and were shaking their slow heads and shaking their slow hands as they conversed and consoled. They were saying the words shame and awful and poor and tragic and trial and no-one and God and better and strong and sudden. The siblings sipped at their lemonades.

'Fucking Irish pricks,' muttered Bernard eventually.

'They're family,' said Shannon.

'Still pricks though,'

'Still family though,' and Shannon stuck out her tongue at her brother.

'Can't wait till they go home. Leave us alone.'

The relatives were peeling away from Patrice and Nandad now and heading toward the bar. One man in a silk waistcoat stopped to pick up a handful of twiglets. When he saw the children watching him, he smiled widely and gave them a low nod.

'It's really beautiful there,' said Shannon.

'Where?' said Bernard.

'Ireland.'

'Have you ever actually been there?

Shannon paused for a moment and looked up at the low ceiling, 'No.'

'Well it's shit. Everyone knows it's shit, especially the Irish. That's what Dad says.'

'Well, Mum says different.'

'Yeah, but Mum's a woman.'

'So what?'

And at this Bernard jolted his head back and looked out into the room, as though the argument had been definitively won. But just in case it hadn't actually been definitively won, he added,

'Women always think everything's beautiful, Shan.' And then he stuck his gob around his straw and dragged out the rest of his lemonade.

After she was dead, a change came to the Nacullians. This change was bitty bitty and slim slim, but eventually no-one thought of Betty as the eldest child anymore. Talk about her was frequent at first, at the dinner table, walking home from school, during ad breaks. But the talk became muted, and then unusual, and then only by slippage or accident. This was not because Betty had been forgotten, but because sometimes, it's two o'clock in the afternoon and you've not had your lunch.

CHAPTER SEVEN

The Adventures of Nandad Nacullian
(1996)

Do you remember those Sundays in November when the air was filled with wafers of cold rain and the sky was slung low and brown over the city and dark leaves were mulching down in Palmerston Park? Those Sundays of damp silence and slow breathing when Bitterne High Street was utterly empty save for a few scattered chips dropped the night before?

Ok, so you probably don't remember those Sundays at all, but you could at least use your imagination. On Sundays such as these, Greg would sometimes catch his Grandfather in a good mood after the Sunday roast. Greg knew he was in a good mood because Nandad would respond to questions by saying more than three words. It was on Sundays like these that Greg would ask Nandad questions about the olden days. He would stare in wonder at the incomprehensibility of the pre-decimalised age or the idea of outside toilets. And to be fair, Nandad was pretty engaging.

So settle down, and listen.

Yes. Well. You see now. I'm a man now. Don't you go writing all this down now. Well, I'm a man. I worked with me hands. I worked with me feet and me back like most men. And a man's as much of a man as he can carry on his back. Yes now, that's a good one, and you can write that down for nothing: A man's as much of a man as he can carry on his back.

It was many years ago now I came over, and she came with me. You see now, I saved her you see, I saved my wife and she's never properly thanked me for it. Women are ungrateful, and you can write that down. And if you end up saving a woman from something, she's even more ungrateful to you. Though a man's as much of a man as he can carry on his back, as I've said.

A man's as much of a man as he can carry on his back.

Too right. Now, I was still a young man when I came over and back then I was something. And I mean something. I could drink the Bann dry and I could drink the Lagan empty, that was me. I could ford the seas like a fish and cross the land like a hare. By God, my fists were as big as the Black Mountain then. I'd knock a man down and the man would be staying down. I'd push a man away and the man would be staying away.

Once, I went down to Dublin with me father on some business. To tell the truth, it was on some battle business, some fist business, we went down to Dublin. Down in Dublin there was a fella who'd heard that me fists were as big as the Black Mountain and that if I knocked a man down he'd be staying down. Well, this fella, Benandonner was it? Or maybe Frank, was it? Well, he had heard about me and had wanted to challenge me. But my father was having none of it. No Nacullian's going to be slighted by some Liffey-livered fool he says, no son of mine, he says.

So we met in Clontarf, or it might have been by the docks, I'm not sure. There were crowds like the 12th July, though they might just have been smaller. Now Benandonner now, he's a big man now. A very big man. A giant of a man now. A giant in fact now. His shoulders were the height of old masted ships and his chest was like two barrels strapped together and used as some kind of wee boat. Though they weren't a wee boat, they were a man's chest.

And a small boat is really big for a man's chest.

Well that's obvious, isn't it? It'd only take a slow man to work that one out, wouldn't it? Now listen you. Well, so some fella starts calling out odds, the odds of me knocking this man Benandonner down and him staying down, or the odds of this man besting me, fat chance. This man calling the odds was my father, I think, who had put on his good jacket with the sparkly sequins, which he always did at times like these. And there's wagers being took and taken and some men are throwing down their coins, their paper money, their loot and their jewels to have their part in the show. And soon at my father's feet there's a pile of gold, gold like I'd never seen. Gold as big as the height of old masted ships or a big as the Black Mountain, I swear.

And to make sure of fair play there's a referee called in specially. From Meath, I think. A little wee man that looked a lot like my father, but in a different jacket. He brings us both into him and looks at us hard. Biting, he says, is allowed. Gnawing, he says, is allowed. Kicking, spitting, gouging, grappling, he says, is allowed. Swearing's encouraged. Baiting and slating's required. But if you think about going for a man's balls you can think again. A man's balls are his own private world and no man enters another man's world. We are respectable people, after all. We are civilised people, after all: Now smack the fuckin' shite out o' one another!

So, did you win?

Did I win? Did I win! Course I won. But let's not put it down that simple, now. There's a story being told here that doesn't need you in it, right? Well. Let me see. So, me fists were as big as the Black Mountain and Frank's chest was like a wee boat, which is very large for someone's chest. Ah yes, so the bell rang and the bell ringer was my father, who was standing in for someone else who must've been late.

And so the beginning began. We circled each other to start with, like we were thinking about what would happen next. The men around us were shouting or maybe they were silent-quiet, like it was a solemn occasion. One or the other, certainly. You could smell the salt from the sea and there was malt in the air. Yes, I remember that now. Salt and malt. Make sure you remember that, boy: Salt and malt.

But what's malt, Nandad?

God, nevermind what malt is, just remember it and know it's important.

Now then. Ah! Now after circling, I went in for a jab and Benandonner pulled back. He was a swift man. He went at me for a kick that I knocked away. There's tactics there. Then he lands the first punch on me because I'm blinded by the sun, which I forgot to mention. So I'm caught by a sunray in the face and Frank comes in to lay one in me chest. Imagine now a rock being thrown at you. Imagine now a stack of rocks being thrown at you. A stack of rocks as tall as old masted ships. Like a mountain. Yes, an actual mountain. His punch was a full mountain weight, a mountain's force, in me chest. And I'll admit I stumbled back and there was this hush, because the men round me thought I was done for.

The referee that looked like me father then comes to up to me to check me over and dust me off: 'Lose to him and you'll not eat for a month from my table, I swear,' he says, which is something all referees

63

say to you to encourage you.

So, I walk back towards this Frank fella and I can tell by the look of him he's surprised I'm still taking air. And I can tell by the look of him he's scared. I flex me hands out and because me hands were as big as the Black Mountain. It was a sight to see, I tell you. And then there was this hush, because the men round me thought he was a gonner. There was salt and malt in the air, I remember.

Then what?

Then what? What do you mean, then what? I'm telling you a story here, aren't I? I am the one who tells ye then what and what then, so just shut yer gob and listen. Now, then what? Ah yes. So I hits him and then he hits me. Then he hits me and then I hit him. Then...this carries on for a time, this hitting. And there's still salt and malt in the air there, I vividly remember.

So then I throws an uppercut at him. He dodges to the side. But he's off balance now, I can see. I kick out with me right leg and he's down in the muck, right down where he belongs. But not for long. Up he comes this Benandonner-Frank fella and yer man's throwing punches and kicks and spits and gouges at me like there's no tomorrow. My hands are going like this and like that, this way and that way, defending meself from himself like there's no tomorrow.

And now though, I'm driven back towards the crowd and...

But why didn't he stay down?

What now?

He went down. When you knock a man down, he stays down. But he didn't.

Well. Well I see you're listening and remembering, so that's good. But you're not so smart, mister. Because that's not how it went. Remember now that Benandonner's a giant and not a man like most men, so he's not likely to stay down. And yes, and that's it yes, I kicked

*him see and a kick and a punch are two different things, so that's
that. So, little eejit, you just listen to what I'm tellin' you a little more
and be interrupting a little less.*

So where am I now?

I said, where was I now? You made me forget.

I'm not meant to interrupt.

*Ah forget that nonsense now and just tell me where we left off, if
that dundered head of yours can do any remembering.*

There's no tomorrow.

What now?

Where we left off. You said there was no tomorrow.

*Was that it now? There was no tomorrow? No, no there was a
tomorrow because I was defending meself like there's no tomorrow.
That's it. Well now. The crowd goes quiet now. The crowd hushed.
Malt and salt. Me and Benandonner in a grapple hold, our strengths
opposed, our wills opposed. Spitting. Swearing. Trying to gouge one
another, trying to gore one another. But respecting each other's balls,
each other's private worlds. Two men there then, respecting each
other's balls.*

*But we're tiring now see and the sun is hot. Hotness like the tallness
of old masted ships. Hot like some mountain that's very hot for some
reason. And I'm moving me hand out from around Frank, I'm getting
me hand out from round his back and I'm raising it into the air. I can
hear him breathing. I can hear me breathing. I can hear someone
that sounds like me father encouraging me on by threatening me with
starvation. My hand's about to strike.*

*When just at that moment some Guard comes over and peels us
off one another, just as I'm about to strike the man down. I look this
Guard in the face and see he's the spit of me own father and then
he tells us all that this fist business is done and over with. Illegal,*

see. No licences, he says. No permits, he says. No whatsamecallits. Pack up and go home, he says. I'm confiscating the winnings, he says, illegal winnings and by rights I should have the whole lot of you locked up.

So there's a great hush now, a great hush because all the people have scarpered at seeing the Guard. And...

But, Nandad, you said you won?

Oh, this sounds about right, doesn't it? More questions. Well, as a matter of fact that's true, I did say I won. I can see you're paying attention. But you see, I was about to win when everything was called off, so...

So, you didn't actually win?

Yes I did, I did actually win, certainly and no question. But when a man's about to win without actually winning, it's called a moral victory. What I won was a moral victory, a real actual honest-to-god moral victory. And I was the happier for it.

Oh.

Didn't bank on that one, did ye? Didn't see the moral victory creeping up on ye while you were asking all the questions. And let me tell you something else. Soon after, Benandonner-Frank, see he gets wind of this real actual honest-to-god moral victory of mine and he's raging. He would have preferred I got an actual victory over him rather than this great moral victory of mine, so he's not a happy man. And he knows people. And some of those people he knows know people who know people who know me and so like, coward like, he goes for me. He gets his friends to go for me and they enter my world, my private world and no man should be entering another man's world.

What did they do to you, Nandad?

Well, I swore to Nanny I'd not go into details, but after they entered my world I knew I had to leave, for they'd keep coming into my world until I didn't have a world left at all. By this time now I had a wife, because she had heard about this moral victory of mine and had fallen in love with me, oh so in love. Love like there's no tomorrow. Love like the tallness of old masted ships. So, I married her, and funny thing, the Priest could have been my father's twin, I swear. I saved her you see, I saved my wife and she's never properly thanked me for it. Women are ungrateful, and if you end up saving a woman from something, then she's even more ungrateful to you.

But being my wife, she had to leave with me, and so she went with me. We started out in Carlingford Loch, paddling, like. It's possible we'd just been having a picnic. It's possible it was cheese sandwiches and tea, or maybe it was wild honey and salmon. Anyway, she latched her arms over me back like a necklace, like a cape, and whispered for me to save her, to leave the place and to save her. So, I started swimming out, my great big hands making short work of the water. It was well known that when I pushed water aside it stays pushed aside.

I was that fast a swimmer that within an hour we were near the Isle of Man. We come so close we could hear some of the Manx shouting at us, but they're shouting in Manxish, so I didn't know what they were on about. But they must've been angry, cause soon they're throwing these rocks at us, or was it life rings, maybe? Ah, well whatever it was, I picked up me pace and me hands were as big as the Black Mountain, so when I pushed the sea aside it stayed aside. We soon left those Manx and their shouting behind.

And then you got to England?

Wait wait, not as simple as that, for Godssakes. The problem with you's that you don't know what a good story is. Now, I'm telling you this now for your own good. Give a tale time to brew. Let the cheese melt a little in the sarnie before you eat it. Stop pushing now and listen. Now, where am I heading to now?

To the city?

Aye of course to the city. But it was a long trip. A long and arduous trip. Might have gone to Liverpool and got the train down, but no, a train would have been slower because when I pushed back the waves, the waves stayed pushed back. Me wife was on me back, straddled over me back like a back of bacon she was. Now, I would have walked across the seabed see, but the wife wasn't the kind to be taking a drink of the salt water, so I kept her up all the way, round me back like a necklace, like a cape, like a back of bacon. But like I always say, a man's as much of a man as he can carry on his back.

The night passed in darkness and the dawn passed in pinkness. Yes, that's a nice way of putting it. We had gone past Wales and round the arm of Cornwall and then on. And then it was day and I knew we were close because I could see my hands getting smaller and smaller, closer and closer to the size of a man's hand, just a normal man's hands. I knew then we didn't have long to reach the city.

On my left, I saw the land England and then on my right I saw the Isle of Wight and then I took a left and I swam up, up through the Solent and towards the city. I'll admit it was heavy going. By this time me hands didn't look like the Black Mountain at all. They looked just like a swollen pair of hands. And my wife didn't look like a necklace at all, but like a woman who'd have preferred to have taken the train. And in the docks there, there were these old masted ships that were as tall as old masted ships and there was no one throwing rocks or life rings or paying any attention to anything.

What was England like back then?

A lot different. Different from there and here. Different from now. But a man's as much of a man as he can carry on his back. There's lots about it I noticed. For one, there was no one who looked like me father. People in England who refereed fights or rang bells or took bets or married people, they didn't look like my father. No more fathers for me. And in England, my hands were just like any other man's hands. In England, I'd not be drinking the Test dry or the Itchen empty. Suddenly, it'd be a few glasses in me and I'd be fallin' over meself already. And you know that once I got here to the city, I couldn't swim the seas anymore. No more of that for me.

So, I got meself up from the stones on the beach and I thought, 'you're just a man now.' And that's why I look like a normal man to you, because now I'm just a normal man. Why the wife loved it here so much I'll never know, I swear. It's just a normal life here, but maybe it would have been a normal life anywhere, I don't know.

Do you ever want to go back?

Ah, that's a question. Yes. Why not go back? Why not? Well, you might feel this one day, you might know this one day that places can be small. It doesn't really matter if they're actually small or actually large, but any place can feel small. And that place back then, to me, felt small. That, of course, and the fact that the Protestants cut a hole in me prick.

But that's another story.

CHAPTER EIGHT

An Interlude about Parks

It's about time we took another little break from the Nacullians and broadened our gaze from the shint and chiver of their lives. You'll remember that a while ago I welcomed you to the city and promised you'd drive along the city's roads, stroll through its parks, taste the air and that kind of thing. Well, you should know by now that I keep my word. So, welcome to an interlude about parks. Cue music.

Now, did you know that the city has some beautiful parks and green spaces? Well, if you're from the city then you probably know that, but you probably don't know that if you're from Seoul or Baku or Portsmouth. So, let me give you a little tour.

Yes, the city has many parks and green spaces. To name a few: Mayflower Park, Mayfield Park, The Common, East Park, Veracity Rec, Palmerston Park, Houndwell Park, Hinkler Green, Watts Park, Queens Park and many more besides. Some parks are the pompous acts of history and some parks were the benevolent plans of politicians. Some green spaces are what's left behind after the wildfire of urbanisation and some spaces are the splinters of once-great estates. Though while the city has its parks and green spaces, it's hardly the kind of city anyone comes to for that reason.

Perhaps this is because of the fact that while the city has its parks, one thing it doesn't have is parkish parks. By parkish parks, I mean the kind of park that's a place for itself, in itself. When you enter a parkish park, you enter a domain, a place with its own circumference and separation from the city surrounding it. Go to London and you roam and frolic in Hyde Park and somehow, you're not in London, not in the city anymore. Go to Dublin and you get lost and exhausted in Phoenix Park, like Nandad did in 1947. And whilst you're lost and exhausted in Phoenix Park, you're not in Dublin, not in the city anymore. It's this kind of park that my city lacks, so you know that when you're in the city's parks, you are always still in the city.

But of course, while this is the case, parks are not one thing always. They shift with the season. In the summer in Palmerston Park or East Park, yes, there are gaudy flowers on raised beds and gaudy ice-lollies from vans. Teenagers hunker down behind bushes and they paw and scrape around each other's mouths and genitals, searching for adulthood. Small children in council-maintained sandpits paw and scrape at the yellow dirt, searching for Australia. Saturday-Dads pushing their kids on swings paw and scrape their offspring's backs, thinking about their estranged partners with jealousy and despair. Only a tourist like Kate-or-Rose who dreams of the RMS Titanic and the lore surrounding it does not paw and scrape. She just sits on her coat in the sunny park and thinks about her flight to Cork, the city which was the last stop of the RMS Titanic before the ill-fated ship continued on its ill-fated voyage blah blah blah.

Then there's the autumn, which starts off by pawing and

scraping at the teenage body of summer. Though soon things begin to sag and wrinkle, and citizens forsake these spaces as Houndwell Park and Veracity Rec dampen and mulch into the humus of the year. Heroin addicts begin to die on dark wooden benches. Park rangers and gardeners quietly push the cooling leafslurry into corners, or drive it away in vans with cages at their rear. And if you were very lucky, once in the Autumn of 1983 you might have caught Bernard Nacullian masturbating to a scrap of pornography he found by the bushes in East Park.

And in winter, fingers of sable trees line Watts Park and Hinkler Green. The parks in winter are not the frost-filled or snow-softened sentiments you would find in postcards, no. A winter park in this city is a limp, anaemic thing, a testament only to its own obsolescence. It is destitute even of the destitute, who have died or been pushed into corners or driven away in vans with cages at their rear. Gardeners and attendants wander about with pincering litter-pickers and they empty half-empty bins into larger half-empty bins and then drive them away in vans with cages at their rear.

Then finally spring comes, crippled and quavering into Mayfield Park or The Common. Addicts appear again on dark wooden benches and park rangers test out their mowers and chippers and strimmers. Spring in the city's parks is a kind of gathering together of the rest of the year. Spring has the damp of the autumn and the treefingers of winter and it has the gaudy flowers of summer. If you pawed and scraped around searching for the essence of the year, you would most likely find it in springtime by the bushes in East Park.

Though a year in the life of a city park is far more than a story of seasons. It's a story of people too, or maybe the lack of them.

Because people are really only in the parks during summer and in the scraps of time that hang off of summer. For more than half the year, parks are little more than the paths that cross them or a place to let your dog have a sly shit in or to shoot up in or to die in.

Why not build houses on parks then, which could be lived in for the whole year? Why not build an orphanage on the park, to give the poor little children somewhere to call their own? Why not erect a shelter there to keep the poor little destitutes warm during the bitter nights? Maybe a cathouse to protect the poor little kitties or a doghouse to protect the poor little doggies?

It must be that parks are strictly speaking, excessive. And you know that this city has many beautiful parks and green spaces. The city then is a city of excess, and this is why the parks must remain in the city. This is exactly why I'd sit myself down in front of a steamroller in Palmerston Park to stop the cathouse being built. It's exactly why I'd burn down the orphanage if even a slip of it was erected on Mayflower Park. Sod the totally necessary shelters and orphanages and cat homes and dog sanctuaries. Hurrah I say for the excesses of Palmerston Park and Hinkler Green. So, hurrah I say for the places where people paw and scrape.

And if you happen to be from a place without parks, well, doubtless all of this will seem excessive, and you'll be wondering what I'm getting so worked up about. And to you, I'd say that a city with no parks doesn't need parks, for the tone has already been set. Work here, die here, visit the country at weekends. It's only the cities with parks that need them.

What then does this mean about parks and the city? To put it like a sentimentalist, parks really are hope. To put it like a cynic, hope is just unfulfilled sentiment. To put it like the realist, cynicism is the refusal to hope, which will never actually stop you hoping. And to put it like a park ranger, there's dog shit over there needs cleaning up.

CHAPTER NINE

The Ward Singer
(2011)

Every Tuesday and Friday, Belinda Watson volunteered at the General, singing hits of the 1980s to stroke victims. She had picked up a glossy NHS leaflet about it once, after her regular slot at The Garden Wall and supposed that playing to the very ill wasn't so far off playing to the very pissed. Just after the one o'clock lunch round, Bel would bulge out of one of the central lifts with her equipment and squeak left down the long oblong corridor towards F-Wing. When she entered through the double-doors, the nurses' confetti of smiles and chat fluttered around her as they glided from ward to ward.

'Hello Bel!'

'Play that one from last week, will you?'

'Shannon's teary today...'

'Watch out for the mess in Ward C!'

'Mrs J is lucid for once.'

'Non-stop non-stopnonstop...'

F-Wing had four wards, and Bel always began with the middle C, for no other reason than this was where she had first played on her first day volunteering. Apparently, a patient had spent the long night ranting about Phil Collins and 'Something Happened on the Way to Heaven' and one of the nurses had asked if she knew that one.

Bel had said that, yes, she knew the song, and she set herself up on her stool in the white ward's white centre. When she jiggled over the opening riff and strummed the A Flat Major 7th chord, a previously twitching patient stilled and raised her thinly-haired head.

♪ *We had a life, we had a love* ♫
♫ *But you don't know what you've got 'til you lose it (Ooo,ooo)* ♪
♪ *Well that was then, and this is now...* ♫

This must be the patient the nurses had whispered of, Bel had thought. As she played it through, coyly, but with enough energy to hit the notes, the woman's eyes widened and her tawnythin hair lifted, as if by a breeze. Though when the song was over and Bel segued into 'Lady in Red', the patient turned away and began to moan, just as before.

'Mrs Alsaid, what can I do for you?' A preternaturally chirpy nurse strolled over to the fidgeting form by the window. The patient moved her tacky sagging mouth up and down, uttering the tones of the terribly ill: Gung, hoow, oose, naaa. She raised her left hand above her and with a three-fingered point, gestured towards a cup of orange liquid on the overbed table.

'Ah yes, let's get you something to drink,' said the nurse, as he brought a straw to the patient's lips.

After Ward C, Bel worked her way to D, looped back to A and then finished with Ward B. It would have been easier to have played the same songs for each ward but the nurses' constant movements made her wary of repetition. As a compromise, for each ward she swapped an old song for a new. Bel felt happiest playing Ward D, because she had loosened up and her fingers and wrists moved fluidly and with assurance. But it was her last performance in B that was always a struggle, as the work seemed somehow done before it had properly ended.

Though she'd been playing at the General for some time now, she still maintained an interest, as she had learned that this gig required skills not needed for punters down The Garden Wall. For example, against the background moans and gurgling profanities Bel had had to find the perfect volume where the music would neither drown out the patients, nor be drowned by them. It did not matter if she was singing 'Total Eclipse of the Heart', 'Turn Back Time' or 'I Want to Know What Love is', the audience had a right to be present, even if they didn't know Bel existed, and was singing to them.

As she settled into the routine of playing and moving and playing again, slow and certain things had become apparent. What first appeared to be chaos on the ward was nothing of the kind. Yes, the patients radiated chaos, because illness is chaos, but the staff had a slowness even in panic and a mildness in their sighs which said everything was under control. No, a ward was not simply a room with beds and machines and the sick and the dying and the dead. Each ward had a subtle topography. Bel had noticed that often, those who died were placed in the middle of the room, but those by the windows were more often than not discharged, having partly rebuilt their crumbled cognition. Why this was, was unclear. Perhaps the weak sunlight that would grapple onto the windowsill in the afternoons offered some comfort, or maybe it was the vista of the city outside, squat and formless, reminding the patient of home.

Bel only thought about things like this when she wasn't at the General, because as every musician knows, thinking too much as you play will lead to mistakes. Ask yourself what time signature you're playing in and you'll be out of time quicker than stroke victims promote sympathy. And if you wonder about the number of sharps in the key of F# Major as you're rocking out to 'I Want to Know What Love Is', then well, you certainly won't end up finding out what love is. Either a thing was done or it was not done and considerations of the time signatures and the keys of life were for later, at home.

Home was a small flat in a staved suburb on the outskirts of Bitterne. There, Bel often wondered why she only ever played to stroke victims. Maybe she had missed a different glossy NHS leaflet at The Garden Wall. At any given time, she imagined, there might be a dozen or so ward singers at the General, performing to different ailments as their genre dictated. Fat men playing slow disco in oncology, a Prog duo changing key and time signature more than was necessary in neurology, a lone little girl singing a cappella folksong in geriatrics. Perhaps it was just the stroke wards that needed pop songs with a rock tinge from the 1980s.

'Gerroff! You...bastard. You bloody, oh, you bloody bastard. Bloody bastard shit! Help meeeee...!'

Avril was being difficult. Bel had just folded out her stool and unpacked her instruments when Avril vomited up a tuna and mayo sandwich back onto her plate. When the nurses rushed to help her, whipping round the curtain as a shield of dignity, Avril had sensed only the shadow of destruction upon her. And to the shadow of destruction, she replied, 'Oh, you shits, you fffff; you brutes. No! Mummy! Dad, Dad tell them, No!'

Bel had seen her this way before, whenever that wrinkle of a body needed help. Avril would scream and cry and spout the curse words and the naughty things she had heard whilst pretending to be asleep in the 1940s. She never listened to Bel's music, and she had been placed squarely in the middle of the ward. Bel imagined Avril at night, sweating and swearing and filled with the scent of doom and cold piss.

Behind Avril's curtain, the noises quelled and Bel passed an opening smile around Ward C. She began with a softly arpeggiated rendition of 'Eye of the Tiger', and she caught herself thinking that played this way, the song was unfamiliar, even to herself.

♫ *So many times it happens too fast* ♪
♪ *You trade your passion for glory* ♫
♫ *Don't lose your grip on the dreams of the past...* ♪

Some songs are this way, with the overfamiliar being initially alien. But then, once you recognise the song you are relieved, you calm, you attune. A thing is done, or it is not done. When this happened and uncomprehending eyes suddenly became focussed, Bel felt freer, as if the song and not the player was there. And today, the new woman focussing on her was Shannon Nacullian, a plumpish and pale-eyed woman Bel supposed was somewhere in the flats and sharps of her forties. Bel noted that Shannon had been placed, auspiciously, next to the large window at the end of the ward. Directly looking at Bel, she mouthed along to the song, sticky-lipped and hollow-eyed, as though she might be looking at a television.

When the song was over, Shannon half-smiled and patted the bed with one hand in applause, her other being contorted beneath her breasts. Bel nodded in Shannon's direction, and then slowly moved into the next ballad.

It had been about four weeks since Shannon had been brought in, having suffered a volley of small stokes, which the doctors said added up to a large stoke. Like most people who have wormed their way out of the tunnels of delirium only to find themselves in the General, Shannon had been inconsolable at first. When seconds later after waking, the extent of her paralysis became clear, she was less consolable still.

Shannon was attended most by the pale-eyed, plumpish form of Greg, who always brought chocolates and usually ended up eating them himself. When he had visited her just after the stroke, he was full of awkward kisses and constant nodding at her gungs, hoowses, ooses and naaas. But as a semblance of progress progressed, Greg became less panicked and would quickly find himself without much to say or do during his visits, so he would sit there thumbing away at a phone as he furtively ate the chocolates he'd left on top of Shannon's side cabinet. While Greg's boredom reflected a kind of dull hope for his mother, Shannon herself could only adopt a method of mourning, as though her life was already over, before it had ended.

Shannon hadn't experienced anything like this since childhood. Not that she had had a stroke as a child, but she remembered that so often when she was a child, she had found it impossible to be satisfied. Once when she was very young, the family had been eating one of Patrice's giant brown stews and Shannon was whinging for another dumpling. Eventually, Patrice gave in and plopped her own last dumpling into her daughter's bowl, but it was not enough. Child-Shannon saw that, yes, she had got what she'd wanted, but it still wasn't enough and somehow, it was never going to be enough.

Life directly after her stroke was like this. Existence was an endless series of wishes that once granted, were taken down to the riverbank and drowned by bigger wishes.

At first for example, all she wanted was to be able to move her left hand, just to move her hand so she could reach for a drink to quench herself.

One day soon after this wish, Shannon could move her hand.

Then all she wanted was to walk, just a few steps, just walk a little down the long white disinfected corridor. How great that would be.

And one day soon after this wish, she was able to walk a few steps.

Then after this, all she wanted was to use the toilet, just take a shit and maybe wipe herself without someone there to steady her and rub toilet paper between the cheeks of her fattening arse. And of course, one day soon after this wish, Shannon managed take a crap on her own, and to wipe herself by herself.

All of this was a torrent of success. But it still wasn't enough and somehow, it was never going to be enough.

It was a Tuesday again.

Belinda Watson bulged out of the central lift with her equipment and squeaked left down the long oblong corridor towards F-Wing. She was a little early and so took her time, observing the celerity and oscillations of the General.

It's a fact that the hallways, gardens and shops of hospitals are some of the least normal of places, a drip tray of limbo, circus and soap opera. Once, Bel had seen some mush dressed as a giant molar giving out samples of toothpaste and armed with a giant cardboard toothbrush. After a while, the massive tooth trotted into WH Smith to buy cigarettes, but the costume was so large that it kept knocking over promotional placards and sweeping racks of chewing gum onto the floor. Exasperated, the shop assistant demanded the molar wait outside whilst being served. Things ended in disappointment though when I.D. was demanded, and the molar patted itself down embarrassedly, before managing a defeated shrug. Sometimes there just aren't enough cavities.

As she dawdled, Bel hummed the melodies of pop songs with a rock tinge from the 1980s. When she turned the corner leading down into the F-Wing, she noticed the plump paleness of Shannon's son trundling towards her. Beside him was Shannon herself, shuffling half-steady, her face doodled over with lines of intense effort. Both of their eyes were fixed on the white disinfected floor, watching each of Shannon's steps as though they were a novelty, as though they were someone else's. Bel smiled at them as she passed, though went unnoticed.

Her pace slowed as she approached F-Wing's windowed double doors. With a shoulder, she eased one door open and made her way through and then into ward C. The first thing she noticed was the middle bed, Avril's bed. It was empty, and the whiteboard holding her name had been wiped clean.

Bel began to unpack and set up, but she was aware that she was distracted. She was thinking about Avril, was thinking about Shannon and every musician knows that thinking too much as you play will lead to mistakes. She sat down on her stool in the ward's white centre. Either a thing was done or it was not done. She picked up her guitar from its stand, felt the strings, the curve of the cool body.

The double doors to the ward were opening. It was Shannon and Greg. Shannon wheezing and leaning on the arm of Greg. Bel watched them as they made their way towards the bed by the window where outside, the city sat squat and formless.

Bel told herself she should not be thinking. She sighed. Something is done, or not done. She paused. She smiled to the room. Avril's bed was in front of her. She played.

♫ *We are strong* ♪
♪ *No one can tell us we're wrong* ♫
♫ *Searching our hearts for so long...* ♪

But she was still thinking. And the lyrics and the chord transitions and the pull-offs and hammer-ons and the vocal line and verse-chorus-verse were a twitching and hobbling and heavy thing, that clinged to her. She heard the words she sang as if they were text behind her eyes. What did this sentence mean? Why was that rhyme chosen? What were the promises of pop tunes with a rock tinge from the 1980s? And what was the reality of the empty bed? What was the reality of Shannon Nacullian, hand-held, step-shattered and elbow-holstered?

The music was tilting now, sagging now, losing balance, and some in ward C were noticing. A nurse sliding a forkful of shepherd's pie into a patient's mouth turned around. As he pulled Shannon's slippers from her feet, Greg glanced over. The performance was over before it had finished, but Bel had to sing on. As she did, she could hear the gargles and titterings that were the ward's own music. Gung, hoow, oose, naaa. As she faltered her way through Pat Benatar, she felt that this music, this ward music, had now become her own.

As Greg helped Shannon into her bed by the window which looked out onto the city, the ward singer finished the song and went formlessly into the next.

CHAPTER TEN

Common Bond
(1988)

With some things, it is impossible to say when they happen. This doesn't mean they don't happen, it's just that we only ever notice that some things have happened after they've actually happened, if you follow me. Love is one of those things, and so is Carbon Monoxide poisoning. And so is the ending of grief. We wake up one morning and check ourselves over and we realise the grief is gone. We're surprised because we hadn't noticed it before, but we notice now that it had happened already. That it happened behind our backs. Maybe it happened in the night when we were sleeping or maybe it happened in the days and weeks beforehand, when our thoughts were on lovers or on our boilers being serviced or on what sandwiches we were having for lunch that day. However it happened, sometimes we find that something has quietly cemented in our lives.

The reason I'm telling you this is because once upon a time, Bernard found himself in a car with his father, as they drove across the city. Nandad had a white 1981 Vauxhall Cavalier with red leatherette seats that burned your arse in the summer, but it wasn't summer. The two had swaddled themselves in thick hi-vis bomber jackets and large black workboots, which Nandad had thrown down on the kitchen table the night before.

'Got you a job and we're both going to the General tomorrow,' he said to Bernard. And that was all he said.

They had passed the Itchen bridge toll booths, were past the central station and had just started on the long and interminable strip of road that was Shirley High Street. After this they would be at the General Hospital, where a new wing was slowly being erected. The two had been silent for about half an hour, a silence which had begun when they were still outside the house. Bernard had flicked on to Radio Solent, 96.1 FM, where the Bee Gees were singing loud and proud about the depth of love or something. No Bee Gees fan himself, Bernard spun the dial amid bubbles of screechstatic before Nandad snapped, 'Turn that off.' And that was all he said.

Bernard knew about the silences of his family and he knew to keep quiet until the old man decided to start up again. Besides, he was hardly in the mood for conversation himself. His father had told him nothing about the job at the hospital and the work gear he had got him was on the large side. He could feel his feet spacewalking inside his boots, nowhere near the steel toe-cap. He'd have to ask his mum for thicker socks when they got home tonight.

It was just after they had started up Shirley High Street that Nandad broke the silence. And it wasn't so much as breaking the silence, Bernard considered later, but pretty much a shooting the silence in the head and then burying it in wet cement.

'Now listen Bernard,' Nandad began. 'In this life, you'll meet several kinds of bricks.'

Bernard turned to his father and checked over the compass of his face for some direction. Nandad kept his eyes on the road and went on, 'Most bricks are standard modular bricks. Now that's just the way of things. But ye can turn any brick two ways, the long way and the short way. If ye turn a brick the long way then ye have yer stretcher. A wall made from stretchers're nice an' cheap to put up and they looks broad and sturdy, but that's all bullshit. If ye turn a brick the other way around though, so that it's facing yer, now that's a header. Stretchers and headers, see.'

'I know Dad. I've known 'bout stretchers and headers and jumbo utility bricks for years now. Why you telling me all this?' Bernard rolled his eyes and looked out to the line of passing shops, boxy and tired.

Nandad continued without answering. 'People'll say a header looks small, but it's headers that give you strength in a wall, because there's brick behind connecting with the bricks in front. People don't see the bricks behind though. They just see the bricks in front. Now, you see where I'm heading with all this?'

Bernard did not see where this was heading, but he nodded and looked out to the middle distance of Shirley High Street, which seemed enough to satisfy his father.

'So what kind of a brick am I, you gonna ask? Well, I'm a standard modular now, no doubt about it. And I'm proud of it too. But now, I'd like to think I've turned myself from one way of facing the world to the other way. From a stretcher to a header like. You might not see much of me, but I'm the one adding strength to the wall, though no-one'll be thanking me for it.'

Bernard nodded and looked out to the middle distance of Shirley High Street. This time he pulled lightly at his chin, which seemed enough to satisfy his father.

'Now you probably think you're not a standard modular.

You probably think you're some jumbo utility or something fancy like that. You'll be thinking you're more formidable than the standard brick. You'll be thinking too that there's fewer of you making up the world than yer wee friends of the standard modular class. Am I right?'

Bernard nodded and looked out to the middle distance. Again, he pulled lightly at his chin, but this time his father didn't continue. Bernard took a risk and turned to make eye contact with the old man, to find Nandad was already staring at him, searching the ground plan of his son's features for viable structures.

Bernard nodded vigorously and kneaded his stubbled chin with his thumb and forefinger, though he soon realised that some speech was going to be necessary.

'Yeah Dad, you're right. So, what am I then?' he asked eventually.

Nandad turned his face back to the road.

'You're like yer father. A standard modular. Be proud of it, but know you've got some learning to do. Right now you're face flat-on to the world, if you get me. All the young lads want to look broad to the world, but it only takes a bit of an eye to see an eejit who'll fall down and stay down when ye push at him.'

Thankfully the lights had just changed. They turned right onto Winchester Road and into the Warren. Bernard knew the route from back when Betty had been there, and he knew there wasn't long to go now. This was just as well, because what his Dad was meaning by all this was an absolute mystery to seventeen-year-old Bernard. To be honest, it would also be a mystery to the twenty-seven, thirty, forty and fifty-seven-year-old Bernard too. After that though, he would forget his father had ever talked to him about the metaphysics of bricks.

Still, right now what he did know for sure was that the old man was speaking far more than he had ever heard him speak before. The grains of his father's speech were suddenly turned into a great big beach of speech with arguing families and sleeping drunks getting sunburnt. Another thing he was also fairly sure about was that his father was trying to be fatherly. There was just no other explanation was there? Both the speech and the fatherliness though were rare enough to make Bernard nod and look out to the middle distance and to pull lightly at his chin, even if his father was talking crazy bollocks about bricks.

They had just turned onto the last road before the General. Bernard relaxed a little and wiggled his cold feet inside his boots.

'And last thing,' Nandad said. 'I've been a brickie nearly forty years. I've sweated and I've ached and I've bled, you know. And I've listened and learned when I've had to listen and learn and I've told yerman to go fuck himself when I think yerman needs to go fuck himself. I'm respected in this city and that's something too that I've built.' His gaze was darting between his son and the road now. His hands were sliding up and down the wheel like they were covered in butter. Bernard had never seen his Dad in such a frenzy.

'And I know my business,' Nandad almost sang. 'This Nacullian knows his business. And you know I'll not have my own son embarrassing me by acting like a spalpeen or by playing the eejit. If you shame me out there, you'll not eat for a month from my table, I swear.'

Nandad's hands began to steady. As they turned off Tremona Road and into the pay and display carpark, Bernard continued to nod mildly and hold his chin and look into the middle distance while his father finished speaking to him about being an embarrassment. Nandad didn't speak again until they had parked up and the engine was off.

Things were quieter in the cooling bowels of the carpark. 'That clear?' said his father.

Bernard knew what he had to say, but he stalled.

'I said, that clear?'

It was so unfair. His Dad had told him fuck all about this job, his clothes didn't fit him and then he'd had to listen to some loony bloody drivel about bricks. And now he was an embarrassment. It was just so unfair, but Bernard of course couldn't say it was unfair.

So, in the quiet semi-darkness of the multi-storey carpark Bernard turned his face and said it, that yes Dad, it was clear. His father gave a swift nod and got out of the car. This was what his son should have said to him, this was what he wanted of course, but in his mind he was saying over and over to himself: Feckin' stretcher that boy is.

Nandad and Bernard were walking over a levelled piece of ground towards the site office. When they got there, Nandad asked for the foreman, who was apparently over at the north end inspecting a retaining wall that had been poured yesterday. As they passed through the site, men looked up from their jobs and looked round from their tasks and looked over from their conversations.

'Gary,' said Nandad.

'Nacullian,' said Gary.

'This is my boy, Bernard,' said Nandad.

'Bernard,' said Gary.

'Gary,' said Bernard.

'Sam,' said Nandad.

'Nacullian,' said Sam.

'This is my boy, Bernard,' said Nandad.

'Sam,' said Bernard.

'It's Samson,' said Sam.

They wandered on through the site, Nandad keeping an eye out for the foreman. Bernard had heard his Dad talk at home about this job or that job, but he'd never actually been on site in his life. He realised now that he had always expected he'd end up here, or somewhere like here, but somehow it was only now that he'd noticed the fact. Everything was unfamiliar, though really should it have been, if he had been expecting this all along? But nevertheless it was strange, and Bernard found himself tucking in behind his father and trying not to gaze around too much. The site was a tumult of girders and bricks and tiles and pipes and concrete blocks and metal cables and hardcore and sand and grit and fibreglass and gravel and slag and rebars and stone and all of the coarse and fine aggregates known to humankind.

'Dad?' said Bernard.

'What now?'

'Why do they all call you Nacullian?'

Nandad stopped dead and checked they were out of anyone's earshot.

'Well what else they gonna call me?' he rasped. 'They're sure as fuck not gonna call me Dad, are they now?'

'Well, why don't they just call you your name.'

'Nacullian is my name,' said Nandad. And that was all he said.

They finally found the foreman having a fag next to a pile of rebars.

'Lenny,' said Nandad.

'Nacullian,' said Lenny.

'This is my boy, Bernard,' said Nandad.

'Bernard,' said Lenny.

'Lenny,' said Bernard.

'That's Leonard,' said Lenny.

The three made chit-chat for a while, about the construction schedule, the promise of Le Tissier's right foot, the weather. Bernard was to start as a labourer at the north end and then they'd see how he did from there. For a while, things seemed to be going well and Bernard decided that showing an interest into what it was they were actually building might have been nice.

'So, then. Leonard,' said Bernard. 'What is it that we're actually building here?'

The foreman dropped a look at Nandad and then back to Bernard.

'Ward for people with brain damage,' he said. 'Now get to work.' And he turned and walked off in the direction of the site office. Without further instruction to his son, Nandad followed Lenny, his head slightly dipped.

Bernard learned later that asking what you were building as you built it was something of a faux pas. Apparently every builder knows that thinking about something as do you it leads to mistakes. Stand back and plan a bit when you need to, by all means. But when you're into something with your back and your hands and your arms and your eyes, you concentrate on what's in front of you. And if you can do the job at hand without knowing what it is you're actually building, well then, why do you have to know what you're building?

After a morning of shifting hods full of standard modular bricks from one part of the site to the other for no apparent reason,

Bernard's body was a pustule of ache and quiver. It was just after midday when without comment, men started to move to the complex of grey huts near the Tremona Road entrance. Bernard followed them as quickly as he could, without attempting any talk. As he walked he checked himself over and found a packet of flattened sandwiches in one pocket and his baccy in the other.

When he entered the main mess hut, Bernard spotted his father in a corner with Sam and Gary and some other guy Bernard hadn't met. He put on a brief smile and a brief nod and headed towards them.

'Gary,' said Bernard.

'Bernard,' said Gary.

'Sam. Samson,' said Bernard.

'Hm,' said Sam, and nodded.

'Boy,' said Nacullian.

'Dad,' said Bernard.

'This is my boy, Bernard,' Nandad said to the guy Bernard didn't know.

'Bernard,' said the guy Bernard didn't know.

'Alright mush,' said Bernard.

'Not mush. It's Andy to you, mush,' said Andy.

And Bernard worked his way around the semi-circle of men to find the only free spot between Sam and Andy. After a moment, the conversation of the little group started up again and joined the room's mix of laughter and smoke and warm damp.

'What you got there then?' said Andy.

The question had come suddenly and because Bernard didn't know what it meant, he turned quizzically to find Andy pointing at the clingfilmed packet he had retrieved from his pocket.

Bernard looked down to his sandwiches and then back to

Andy, who was still leaning in with apparent interest.

'Oh. Peanut butter,' Bernard looked again, 'with lettuce.'

He saw his father cringe slightly and then looked around the semicircle. There were a few smirks and guffaws and beyond the immediate company, a few older guys were looking over and nodding their heads sorrowfully.

'Peanut butter is the sandwich of childish cunts,' Nandad was shouting as they drove back through the Warren that evening. 'Can't believe your mother making you peanut-fucking-butter.'

'Well it's what I asked for!'

Nandad smacked the steering wheel, sending the car veering a little to the right.

'Sounds about right,' growled Nandad. And that was all he said.

Bernard learned later that there was a subtle and sensitive sandwich grammar on all building sites. Either you were speaking the Queen's English in sandwich form, or you were speaking gibberish. Ham was fine, obviously, as was cheese. Luncheon meat or fish paste were ok too. Then you had your all-day breakfast and your Ploughman's at the higher end of the menu. And while people would always complain about the smell, egg sarnies were perfectly tolerable in sandwich grammar terms. There was though a long-standing controversy as to the status of coronation chicken. Some of the guys thought that anything savoury with raisins in it was only fit to give Portsmouth people, whereas others cited the significant meat content of the sandwich, along with its royal connotations.

All would have agreed though that peanut butter was absolutely just for kids. Jam and honey likewise. Even marmite on its own was suspect, and lemon curd would probably get you the shit kicked out of you.

'What is it you want in your sandwiches?' Patrice asked Bernard that night after the family had finished dinner.

Bernard winched his eyes towards his father, who was making a roll-up at the table. He wasn't looking up.

'Whatever Dad's having,' said Bernard.

'Sounds about right,' said Nandad as he licked his roll-up with a deft slide of the paper across his tongue. This of course was what his son should be doing. This was what his son should have said, this was what Nandad wanted of course, but in his mind he was saying over and over to himself, Feckin' stretcher that boy is.

The next day Bernard went to work with corned beef and mustard sandwiches with lettuce. Patrice had run out of clingfilm and had wrapped them in some week-old newsprint and had fastened the lot with an elastic band. Bernard hated corned beef and he hated mustard. He hated the corned beef's gristle and spotty whiteness and he hated getting mustard-nose, which he even got with American mustard, which isn't really mustard at all.

But at lunchtime in the portacabin he chewed on the gristly shitty meat and tried to stop the great yellow tsunami of mustard nose from overtaking his senses. He even copied his father in taking the lettuce out of his sandwiches too, even though he quite liked lettuce.

'Feckin' woman and her fuckin' lettuce,' hissed Nandad as he worked through his sandwich.

Bernard nodded and stared into the middle distance as he tried to control the hot drowning sensation provided by the mustard. He could feel a welter of water coming up to his eyes and at the back of his nose, a trail of thin snot had begun to make its way out into the world.

'What you got there today then, junior?' Andy had appeared above him in the middle of the mess, 'Gone for lemon curd this time?'

Bernard looked up at Andy, eyes puckered and mouth tight. A few titters and scoffs came from around the room and Nandad gazed deeply between his embarrassment of a son and his upstanding example of a sandwich. Though by this time there had been a pause in Bernard giving his answer. A pause long enough for a few heads to turn toward them. In all honesty, it was the mustard nose doing its work, but the room sensed a fight brewing. They saw Bernard's silence not as an attempt to control mustard nose, but as cold contempt. And cold contempt took balls.

Chairs squeaked as more men turned around. Andy felt it necessary to repeat his question, though his speech was more tentative and he had shifted his stance to bring himself flat-on to Bernard.

'So. Lemon curd is it?'

No titters this time. No scoffing. Nandad had stopped looking at this sandwich.

Then Bernard cleared his throat and spoke.

'Sorry mush. I had a bit of mustard nose there,' he said.

There was a tiny silence, and then, a couple of the men gave some short, stabby laughs. Then a few more. Andy looked around and saw this and as if by reflex, he smiled too. A plastered smile. Confused now.

Bernard didn't really know what he had done, but what he did know most definitely was that he was gaining the upper hand.

Somehow and inexplicably, he was gaining the upper hand by talking about his experience of eating his sandwich. He took a chance. He turned to his father.

'Hey Dad, we don't like our lettuce. Maybe this Andy's on the lookout for some?' and in one fluid movement he flicked up a floppy buttered lettuce leaf into the face of his opponent.

Without a script to guide him, Andy grimaced, blanched and took a step backward. No, not a step, they would say later, but a stumble. Yes, definitely a stumble. Smiles came among the men now, and a second later the room chortled as one. And though Nandad himself didn't know what the hell had gone on, he laughed away anyway, because Nandad knew when to listen and learn.

'Scared of a little lettuce, Andy?'

'Only a bloody leaf!'

'Kid got you there, mush.'

'Don't worry, I'm a little scared of lettuce meself!'

That evening on the way home, the two listened to Radio Solent and made the odd comment about bricks and turnbuckles and the fact that Lenny had a cocaine habit. The next day they had fish paste and lettuce.

Then one day, this happened.

'Gary,' said Nandad.

'Nacullian,' said Gary.

'Sam,' said Nandad.

'Nacullian,' said Sam.

'Gary,' said Bernard.

'Bern,' said Gary.

'Sam,' said Bernard.

'Bern,' said Sam.

CHAPTER ELEVEN

Mice
(2015)

Thankfully, the flat was on the ground floor so she didn't have to move. Outside, the main road leading into the city centre buzzed past, never quiet. It had always annoyed her before, but after she got back, Shannon was glad of the continuous thrum of activity.

Shannon Nacullian had spent seven weeks in hospital. During that time, she had learned about a lot of things. She had learned about the ineffable mechanics of walking, of how to reach for a cup and bring it to your mouth, of how to feed yourself. She had learned the skill of loosening your bowels at the right time, and of forcing a strange spaghetti of markings into letters, then letters into words. It was not that Shannon had forgotten all these things that upset her, it was the reminder that these things had to be learned at all.

After her stroke, it was decided that Shannon couldn't be coping alone. But tick, she was on the ground floor and tick, she had her son at home and tick, the OTs were happy she could make a brew without scalding her face off. But tock, she had made slow progress and tock, she was judged to be depressed and tock, her son seemed like a useless piece of shite, according to the social

98

services report. But tick-tock she couldn't sit in bed forever and tick-tock there were new patients all the time and tick-tock, she was keen to go home. So, she was sent home.

Strokes are funny things, and they do funny things to people. I heard once that some total grouchy ornery bastard from Portsmouth became the nicest man you could want to meet after his stroke. Before his stroke he would go about with a little stick, hitting dogs on their noses and knocking children into roads. After the stroke, this guy got himself a dog from the rescue centre and then adopted this refugee kid with only one hand from South Sudan. And another one I heard about was this woman from Totton who after her stroke could play the xylophone like a pro, even though she hadn't touched one since primary school.

For Shannon Nacullian though, the matter was different. True, Shannon had learned a lot in hospital, but she hadn't quite learned to speak, and after her stroke, she could only say one word. And that word was 'mice'. Here's the kind of thing I mean.

'Mice mice,' she would say when she meant, 'Yes, I'd love a cup of tea.'

And, 'Mice is mice,' she would say when she meant, 'Two sugars and little milk'.

Also, 'Mice is micemice mice,' she would say when she meant, 'No, I said two sugars and a little milk.'

And when the ward singer came in to the General to serenade patients with Pat Benatar's 'Love is a Battlefield' and other pop tunes with a rock tinge from the 1980s, you can imagine how Shannon sang along.

There was a fascinating neurological explanation for all of this, but I don't want to include it here because when you go into too much technical detail, readers think you're unfeeling, and this narrator is not unfeeling at all. If anyone is interested, it has something to do with the hippocampus and the amygdala and the pre-frontal lobes, so I heard. And blood clots too, of course. But like I say, that's getting too technical and I'll be damned if I'm going to be accused of being unfeeling.

Apart from her speech though Shannon was surprisingly spry, which is a word we all use when decrepit people surprise us by acting normal. Shannon could hobble about her little two-bedroom flat without falling over much at all. She held her left hand close into her bosom, like a sleeping dachshund, and was even able now and again to winch it out to close a door or slam a window shut. Other than everything that wasn't normal, everything was pretty much normal, and it would be fair to call Shannon Nacullian spry.

On occasion, Shannon gave herself the odd black eye as she made her way around the flat. When the social workers or nurses asked where the black eye came from, she wished she could say 'I walked into the door', instead of 'Micey mice,' because for once the cliché was true, she really did walk into the odd door and it really did give her the odd black eye.

The son, Greg, was still with her, but he generally kept to his room, doing what, Shannon didn't want to imagine. While now in his thirties, Greg was the kind of milk-soppy mummy's boy she both despised and felt a searing and unquenchable maternity towards. He was a jobless jobsworth, overweight and under-nourished, over-stimulated and under-qualified. As far as Shannon knew he had never had a girlfriend since Manu Alsaid in year 5. While she knew that being gay was the clichéd explanation for male singledom, she couldn't help leaning into it like a Zimmer frame, because clichés seem to explain so much and with so little effort. She didn't like the idea of him bringing boyfriends back though, and he didn't, so if he was gay, he wasn't very gay, she reasoned. Can you be half gay, like you can be half Somali or halfway between Bitterne and town? Shannon wasn't sure, so she resolved not to think about it.

She often wished he would move out, but if Greg had left she knew she'd not be able to cope because after every crash, bang, wallop or splat, he would be there, already out of breath from running the few metres between his room and wherever Shannon was sprawled across the floor. The flat, with its doorways and its doors and its radiators and its table edges, had become a hazardous place, no matter how many people told Shannon she was spry.

As well as breakdown service Greg also provided Shannon with something approaching conversation. At mealtimes the son would plop himself down in front of his steaming macaroni cheese and stare at Shannon across their little pine dinner table.

'How are you then, Mum?'

'Mice.'

'Sleeping ok?'

'Mice is mice.'

A squeak of fork on plate.

'Must be annoying, not being able to speak,' said Greg.

Shannon's eyes narrowed and she took a glug of tea.

'Mice mice mice,' she said.

And that was usually the end of it. Greg would schlep back off into his room to leave his mother to do the washing up singlehanded, literally.

It wasn't just the son though, as there was care in the

community. By this I don't mean that people in the community actually cared, but twice a week a nurse would visit to check on Shannon's progress and complain about tripping hazards in the flat. The nurses were nearly always different. English, Polish, Irish, Nigerian, Romanian, Filipino, Portuguese. They were all very friendly, all very busy and Shannon would resolutely shake her head when they asked her if she had fallen recently. They noted down her bruises and swellings all the same, and as they scribbled Shannon worried about the opinion they might be forming of her son.

They would also make her do these silly little exercises, to lift her arms this way, move her leg that way, twist her body like this, bend her back like that. Shannon was meant to do these exercises daily and she always nodded a promise that she would, and always nodded that she had been doing them between visits. The nurses scribbled away all the same.

Sometimes Shannon was unhappy. When she was feeling glum, she would skip having biscuits with her tea and fail to go outside to clean the windows with her yellow sponge-on-a-stick. The nearest she could come to expressing all this glumness was 'mice'. Sometimes Shannon was frustrated, because she had dropped something or broken something or spilled something, and this frustration was mice. Sometimes she would scream out while she was in her bed at night, but there would only be mice. And just on occasion, when she was comfortable in her chair and she saw on the news that some child had been pulled out of rubble or been rescued from a pogrom in South Sudan, she would feel joy. And that joy too would be mice.

Now you might wonder, and you'd be right to wonder, about mice. The word I mean. Why mice? This is something Shannon herself would often wonder about. Why mice? She thought that if this had all been a TV programme or a film or a pop song with a rock tinge from the 1980s, it would have been something much better. TV-film Shannon would be stuck on saying something like, 'Love' or 'My Danny', or 'I know'. Something with a little bit of meaning to it. Sometimes, Shannon would fantasise about being stuck on another word. For example:

'You know how much people love you, now, Shannon.'

'I know.'

And, 'I've got something I need to tell you.'

'I know.'

Also, 'Now, you know you should be doing your exercises every day.'

'I know, I know!'

See? 'I know,' would have worked just fine.

But where did this 'mice' come from? The little grey scurrying things? Shannon honestly hadn't ever given them much of a thought. There was nothing in her life, so far as she could see, that would make her say mice in this kind of a situation. Christ, almost anything would have been better. Like, if she was one of those blokes with Tourette's, at least she could let off a little steam and express a good old cunting fuckady brickbat fuckssake. But alas, she didn't have Tourette's. She even thought she could handle mice if perhaps she said it in another language. Then at least there would be a smattering of dignity about it. She wondered what 'mice' was in French and was sorry she didn't know.

One evening Greg asked for scrambled eggs, baked beans and

spuds for dinner. Nothing unusual there. Shannon responded as usual by starting early, because spuds are a bitch to peel with one hand and scrambled eggs are a bastard to whisk when your bad arm's having to hold down the bowl.

What was unusual was that Greg emerged from his room just before dinner. Because this is what would normally happen:

'Mi-ice!' Shannon would shout down the hallway.

Then, 'There in a minute Ma!' Greg would say, which meant, 'Go away, I'm busy.'

But tonight Greg was early and was sitting down at the little pine kitchen table. He was smiling too and looking directly at Shannon as if he liked her. When she placed his plate of scrambled eggs, fried spuds and baked beans in front of him he leant down to sniff it, actually sniff it, like bad actors do on television.

'Thanks Mum,' he said, which was also unusual.

As the meal began Greg was unusually talkative, as if he was happy or something. He was chatting away about some game of his he played in his room. Had been playing it for years now, he said, which was news to Shannon. It was some game played with others through the wires and cables and satellites and flashing lights and undressing women that made up the internet. These other players could be from anywhere in the world. England, Poland, Ireland, Nigeria, Romania, the Philippines, Portugal. They were his mates, he said. They were his friends, he said.

Greg finished chewing a spud and then swallowed. 'There's this one guy, right, from South Korea. My mate Moon. From Seoul. He calls me Brickim, cause that's my name, like, in the game.'

He was waving his fork towards Shannon, which he never did. Then he started using loads of words and in such a flurry that Shannon didn't have a clue what was happening. Words like

RNG, ragequit, grindfest, avatar, capture-the-flag, rubberband AI, loadout and user interface. Shannon rolled a baked bean about in her mouth. There were then, she noted, some words more ridiculous than 'mice', and there were some words that would have been worse to be stuck with. She considered the following scenario:

'You know how much people love you now, Shannon'.

'Rubberband AI.'

And, 'I've got something I need to tell you.'

'Rubberband AI.'

Also, 'Now, you know you should be doing your exercises every day.'

'Rubberband AI.'

See? 'Rubberband AI,' would have been much worse than 'mice', so every cloud, etc, etc. blah blah blah.

Greg was still gabbing away, waving his fork and using words more ridiculous than mice. Shannon gave the occasional nod and micemice to give the impression she was part of the conversation, but her attention was drifting. She was focussed on her scrambled eggs and was wondering if they were more, or less yellow than when she had made them last time. The scrambled eggs were half finished and the question of their yellowness still undecided when Shannon started paying attention again. Greg was still in full flow, the fried spud on his fork orbiting him like a greasy streaked asteroid:

'So I shot Moon and then Moon shot me. Then Moon shot me and then I shot Moon. Then Moon got pissed off and he nearly shot me, but he didn't because I shot him. Then we both respawn on the next map and I'm right on top of Moon, fragging the fuck out of him and holding one of the chokepoints, racking up the kills. And then we were in the lobby after that and Moon can barely speak English so I'm taking the piss out of him and he doesn't mind, cause he's sound, is Moon. Then he writes something in Korean and I'm like, how the fuck am I meant to understand that, mush? So he goes back to English and I keep on taking the piss out of him. Have you seen those Korean letters? They look like someone put alphabetty spaghetti on acid.'

Shannon put down her fork and picked up her mug for a glug of tea.

'Anyway,' said Greg, 'it was great, Mum. It was really really great. I just wanted to tell you about it.'

Greg took the asteroid out of orbit and crashed it into his mouth. He chewed with big round chews, like someone enjoying a limited edition thingamy on an advert. He was still smiling too. Shannon just looked at him and decided not to say anything. Not that she had anything to say. And not that she could have said anything even if she did have something to say. So, Shannon didn't say anything.

'So,' said Greg, 'what've you got planned tonight then?'

'Mice.'

'Yeah. Well, I think I'll play a bit more. The Yanks'll be online in a few hours.'

'mmmm.'

Greg scooped up a forkful of baked beans, slowly. He looked at his mother and then back to his beans. Little, bitty chews now. More like usual.

He sighed. It was one of those sighs people do on TV when they've made a real effort to be reasonable and kind but have nevertheless been rebuffed. Outside, the main road leading into the city centre buzzed past them. Greg put his fork down in the middle of the plate, which Shannon knew was the sign he was done. He put his hands on the table and started to lift himself up.

But he was stopped. Shannon had swung out her dachshund arm, a finger long and straight and without question pointed at the man across her little pine kitchen table. Greg put his eyebrows together and lowered himself back into his seat. It was then that Shannon said something to her son she had never admitted to anyone.

'Mice. Micey mice is mice. Is mice. Micemice micemice mice. Is mice. Micey is mice mice. Mice! Mice mmmm micey is. Micey. Mmmmmm. Is micey. Micemice. Micemicemice. Mice,' said Shannon.

I could translate this, but there are some things a narrator should leave well alone, because we're an intrusive enough lot as it is. Now please don't go blaming me, thinking I'm some sort of smart-arse who's unfeeling to the world's cruelties or insensitive to the needs of readers and all that. It's not that the world is fundamentally a cruel place or a nice place, or that some narrators are smart-arsed and some narrators insensitive. It is just that the world is a place, and there are narrators in that place. Sure, there are translators too, but they're rarely there when you need them. Do you see what I'm getting at? It would have been much worse if I had told you exactly what she said.

Shannon folded her arm back into place under her breasts and continued with her scrambled eggs, eyes down. Greg stared at his mother. The scraps of eggs and spuds and beans on his plate stared at no one. He opened his mouth as if to say something like, 'What?' or 'Eh?' but was just about quick enough to close it again. As Greg Nacullian rose from the table, America was waking up.

Two weeks later, Greg landed a part-time job at the mini Tescos up the road. His mate Moon however, was far from pleased.

CHAPTER TWELVE

Everi Maner Wight
(1992)

The sea was like a stone. Or perhaps the sea was like a plate of vomit. No, the sea was like the head on a pint of rancid ale. No, it was like the froth in a rabid dog's mouth.

Or maybe the sea was just like the sea.

Patrice, Nandad, Bernard, Shannon and little Greg had got down to the ferry port and had parked up facing the unfamiliar morning water. Not really knowing what to do, they had waited on the concrete amid the colony of other passengers. Over by the edge of Mayfield Park the white box of a burger van had been doing swift business and there was a steady dribble of people leaving the crowd and then returning with floury white baps held in white serviettes. The air was edged with the deep crumbly tang of bacon and the thin bite of granulated coffee. The gulls were above, threatening theft and excrement. By God, it was a beautiful morning.

The ferry was docked and from the terra firma of concrete the Nacullians complained about not being able to just get on the sodding thing, considering it was just there, sitting grey-white, on the sea. After complaining a little more and eyeing the burger van and the people retuning with their baps and Styrofoam cups, people with high-vis jackets and lanyards began to appear. They gestured away and managed to move the small crowd into a line. The line passed by the little green box of a ticket booth and then on towards the thin wooden gangway. Vauxhall Cavaliers and Metros and Escorts began to form a line to the right of the foot passengers, engines quietly ticking over. The morning rush to the island had begun.

Once on board, the Nacullians started off on the main deck with everyone else. As the deck filled, families slowly shifted up the railings to allow others to get one view or another. Greg ran on across the deck and the family followed him toward the front of the ship, where he was jumping up and down on the broad planks to see if he could make the ferry sink.

'I'm a giant!' he shouted, 'My feet are as big as Bitterne leisure centre! Look at me!'

But no-one looked at him. Across the water, a faint line of land loomed.

'That's Wight,' said Bernard.

'Sounds about right,' said Nandad, who was hunched, shoulders-at-ears, on the railings. It was clear to Patrice that he was in one of his sounds-about-right moods. When in one of these moods, he would say sounds about right to almost anything you might imagine. Someone might have called it a sulk, but men do not sulk Nandad would have retorted, they repeat themselves until people stop talking to them. There's a difference there.

This mood had been brought about because of the alarm. Nandad had forgotten to set his highly reliable Bakelite digital clock radio for 6:30 a.m. because he thought Patrice would set it for him. Patrice thought he would set it for himself and Bernard didn't bother setting his alarm because he simply didn't want to get up early on a Saturday to go to the Isle of Wight. Shannon was the only one who actually set her alarm, but her Happy Shopper AA batteries had given out, somewhat mysteriously, she thought.

This lack of alarm-setting had precipitated panic in the Nacullian household, with Nandad flicking awake at 8:07 a.m. and gawping in disbelief at the blood-red numbers on his highly reliable Bakelite digital clock radio. He roused the house by shouting the time the ferry was leaving, which was at 9 a.m., 9 a.m., 9 a.m. and he immediately began to dress. Nandad skipped breakfast and demanded that 9 a.m., 9 a.m. everyone else did too as he rolled his first fag of the 9 a.m. day. He was in such a rush that he did not notice the 9 a.m. blood in his urine or the pint of semi-skimmed milk on the doorstep, which he fucking 9 a.m. kicked over as he dashed toward the car.

'No use crying over that,' snorted Bernard behind him.

Nandad looked down at the white pool that was still spreading over the concrete step, onto and down the gravel driveway. 'Sounds about right,' Nandad said. And so officially, the sounds-about-right-mood had begun.

A little later, they were stuck in traffic by Bitterne leisure centre. Radio Solent was on low and Nandad was staring impassively ahead at the morass of vehicles before him. His fingers tap-addy-tap-tapped on the wheel as he puffed on the tiny flat stub of his rollup.

'Nobody let the dog out for a pee,' observed Shannon from the back.

'Sounds about right,' said Nandad, as the car crawled forward.

'Today, a massive bomb has gone off in the city of London.

Around forty people have been injured and one killed. It is estimated that the bomb may have done up to one billion pounds worth of damage,' Radio Solent said, as they passed over Northam Bridge.

'Sounds about right,' said Nandad, as he fingered his fag butt deep into the already full ashtray.

When they arrived at the ferry terminal, it was 9.07 a.m. and the sky was like a stone. No, the sky was like the head of a pint of rancid ale or the froth in a rabid dog's mouth. Or perhaps it was just like the sky. They all knew they had left things too late really but then so had a throng of other families and individual day-trippers. On top of that, the crew were behind schedule, so all in all they need not have rushed.

'I'm a giant!' shouted Greg again as he stomped around on the deck, 'My feet are as big as Bitterne leisure centre! Look at me, Mum! Look at me Nandad!'

Smoke billowed from the black and red funnel while the rest of the Nacullians ignored Greg. Still busy with trying to sink the ship, little Greg was a little surprised when the horn blasted, well, like a horn. In fact, he was so surprised that he had a little accident, and suddenly stopped trying to sink the ship. He shimmied over toward Shannon and almost immediately, everyone was aware of what had happened.

'Oh, Greg, I thought you were a big boy!'

'Little shit-yer-pants twat.'

'Greg love, what made you go and do a thing like that, now?'

'Sounds about right,' said Nandad.

Shannon grabbed her boy's hand and dragged him off to the toilets below deck. The family shook their heads at the departing mother and child before scanning around to see who else had noticed. To their mutual relief, it seemed the Nacullians had attracted little attention.

As the ferry pulled away the people who started at the back to see the city fade moved to the front of the boat to see the island emerge. The people who began at the front of the boat to see the island emerge shuffled toward the back to see the city fade. Patrice, Nandad and Bernard stared dully back to shore as the ferry clawed over the water, which was like stone, or vomit, or a rabid dog's mouth. There was silence as the city retreated slowly from the boat.

Good afternoon ladies and gentlemen and welcome aboard our Speedsea Yaffle ferry to the Isle of Wight. Your journey today will take approximately one hour and thirty minutes. Conditions are favourable and we are not expecting any problems whatsoever. If we encounter any problems, the crew will advise you of evacuation procedures. In the event of an unlikely disaster, Yaffle ferries operates a women-and-children first policy, but we are not foreseeing any problems, so have a nice trip and see you in Cowes.

The city was nothing more than a sausage of land when Shannon and Greg returned, trying to look as if nothing had happened. Without further comment, the family moved back to the nose of the ship to see how much closer they were to Wight. It would have been exciting if the pitch and roll of the ferry was exiting, but it wasn't, which was why Nandad could roll his fag with ease. It was more like travelling very slowly on a motorway made of water or very slowly on a railway line made of water. Or perhaps it was just like a calm, boring ferry ride to the Isle of Wight.

'What will we do when we get there?' Greg asked.

'Stop asking stupid questions,' snapped Shannon.

'Will there be rides?'

'Tell shit-pants to shut up, Shannon,' said his Uncle Bernard.

'Be quiet Greg. Godssake!'

But Greg's confidence was returning and he was starting back up on his sink-the-ship routine. He began to stamp his feet and rock from side to side.

'Will, will will there be, like, like, like...'

The family gazed harder and further out toward the approaching island. Patrice popped a piece of nicotine gum into her mouth and began to chew. Nandad toked on his rollup and tried to block out his grandchild's chunnering. He thought how much the little eejit annoyed him, and he was even considering breaking his sounds-about-right mood to do something about it. Across, on the starboard side of the deck, a child had fallen over and was screaming, as an unleashed dog pulled at her yellow floral skirt. An adult was rushing over with a rolled-up magazine raised. There were several thick percussive slaps and some dog-yelping.

'Naaandaaaad,' said Greg, 'Didn't Thunder want to come with us?'

Nandad sucked hard on his fag and looked hard at the approaching island, which had now grown from looking like a sausage to looking like an uncooked steak and kidney pie.

'Naaandaaaad,' cooed Greg.

Nandad spun around and looked down upon his grandson. 'D'ye know the Protestants cut a hole in me prick?'

The sea was like a stone. Greg stopped his stamping.

'Godssake Dad, he's only fucking six. Will you stop bloody going on about that!'

Nandad continued to eye the boy, 'Did ye know that?'

Greg gazed up at his Nandad. His feet no longer felt they were the size of Bitterne leisure centre.

'I said to ye, did ye know that?'

'No, Nandad,' responded Greg.

'Sounds about right,' said Nandad, who then nodded and turned away to roll another fag.

Shannon let out a sigh and looked to her mother. Patrice shook her head at no one in particular and then knelt down by her silenced grandson, a dull fifty-pence piece in her hand.

'Look poppit, leave Nandad be and go and find something down in the tuck-shop, will ye?'

As soon as the coin was in his hand Greg was away below deck, leaving the adults to have their adult conversation.

Now, there are comfortable silences and uncomfortable silences in the world. A loving couple after sex, sprawled in linen sheets and covered in dwindling daylight, there's a comfortable silence. Some woman at a rainy bus stop blaming the gays for earthquakes and tornadoes, there's an uncomfortable silence. Then there are Nacullian silences, which are impossibly and somehow in between the comfortable and the uncomfortable, a little like having sex to distract yourself from an ongoing earthquake.

It was Shannon who interrupted the sex-during-earthquake silence.

'D'you know they say you could fit everyone in the world on the Isle of Wright almost exactly?'

Bernard tutted and rolled his eyes the way dickheads do.

'Heard that before, Shan. Not true,' he said as his father passed him a perfectly cylindrical rollup.

'Well, why not?'

Down beneath them, against the blue-black of the ferry's hull, the sea was like a plate of vomit.

Bernard gave another tut and another eye-roll before answering. 'It's the Chinese innit? Do you know how many Chinese there are? There's no way we'd all fit. Now, maybe everyone else apart from the Chinese could fit on the Isle of Wright, but there's no way you could fit everyone and the Chinese on. Stands to reason. What do you think, Dad?'

'Sounds about right,' said Nandad.

Shannon pondered this as she looked down at the vomity slosh below her. 'What if you took the Africans and the Ethiopians off? Do you reckon you could fit the Chinese and everyone else on then?'

Tut. Eyeroll: 'Africans, Ethiopians, they're the same thing, Shannon.' He flicked some ash into the sea below.

'No, they're not. You've got the Africans and then you've got the Ethiopians. I know you Bern, you just think they're all the same.'

'Dad?'

'Sounds about right,' said Nandad. He handed Bernard another perfect rollup, which Bernard slid behind his ear.

Patrice shook her head at no one in particular and then spat her nicotine gum into the sea, which was like the head on a pint of rancid ale. 'Bernard son, just because your father says sounds about right doesn't mean it's right. Stop taking everything he says at face value. You're always doing that. Always did. Isn't that so, Nandad?'

'Sounds about right,' said Nandad.

Bernard let out a little snort but said nothing more. He

reached into his back pocket to produce his own baccy tin and though already well-supplied, he began to roll his own. Someone might have called this a sulk, but men do not sulk Bernard would have retorted, they make rollups. There's a difference there.

For some minutes, there was silence. Cowes ferry terminal was in sight now and from below deck families and singletons emerged, putting on their coats and finishing the sticky iced buns they had purchased below. The girl with the yellow dog-ripped dress had stopped crying and was in deep concentration over a pink Walkman, which she prodded and snapped open, closed, open, closed.

Patrice put another wedge of gum into her gob and zipped up her coat. 'You know,' she said, 'it's just this kind of family time that makes me think of Betty'

'Who's Betty?' asked Greg from behind them. They all spun round. Greg was halfway through an iced bun and held out ten pence change to his grandmother.

'Nanny, who's Betty?' he asked again.

Nandad looked down at his grandchild: 'D'ye know the Prods...'

'Dad! Fuckssake, stop it! He should be able to know who Betty is.'

Patrice bent down and rubbed Greg's shoulder. 'Betty is yer aunty Betty. She left this place before you were even born.'

Nandad had started to edge away down along the chipped iron balustrade.

'Why did she?'

Patrice paused, but kept eye contact with Greg. 'Well, she had to. But even though she left, she loves you and she's watching over you as we speak.' Patrice smiled and pocketed her ten pence change.

This was a lot to take on for Greg. He shot a look up to the sky, which was like a stone, to see if Betty might be there. There were gulls there now, threatening theft and excrement.

Shannon saw the confusion on her son's sticky face as he gawped. 'Greg, Nan doesn't mean Betty's watching over you right here and right now, love.'

'I blummin' well do, you know!' Patrice's words were suddenly spiked and she was now standing. 'Betty's watching us all as we go over to the Isle of Wight for our family outing. She was there this morning when Nandad's alarm didn't go off and she was there when Bernard rolled his first cigarette of the day.'

'God, bet Betty must be bored watching us then,' Bernard sniggered.

'She is not. She loves her family and takes an interest in everything we do.' Patrice gave a firm nod and minced her nicotine gum between her teeth. 'That's my belief, now, that's my true belief. Our Betty takes an interest in everything that we do.'

'Everything?' asked Greg.

'Yes pet, everything.'

There was a lull then and somewhere in the world, people were having sex to distract themselves from an ongoing earthquake. The Nacullians were literally at sea, and I don't mean that in a non-literal way. The horn sounded as the ferry came in toward the terminal and this time, Greg did not shit himself. Shannon looked at her son with a smile of silent pride.

There were people visible on shore now, and some gave the odd wave to those on deck. A queue started to form at the rear of the ship, and the Nacullians followed. After a minute or so, everyone was complaining about not being able to just get off the damn thing, considering the terminal was just there, sitting grey-white, on the concrete. Greg was looking down at his feet, which were starting to grow again toward the size of Bitterne leisure centre. Above them, behind them and in front of them, the tannoy crackled and whined:

Good afternoon ladies and gentlemen and thank you for using our Speedsea Yaffle ferry to the Isle of Wight. The journey has taken approximately one hour and thirty minutes. We were not expecting any problems whatsoever and there were no problems whatsoever. If we had encountered any problems, the crew would have advised you of the evacuation procedures. In the event of an unlikely disaster, Yaffle ferries operated a women-and-children first policy, but we were not foreseeing any problems and there were no problems. So, we hope you had a nice trip, and now we have now arrived in Cowes. We look forward to seeing you again very soon.

Staff in hi-vis jackets appeared again and disembarkation began. The passengers formed into a tightening bundle as they filtered their way down the deck towards the narrow gangway. Nandad flicked his butt into the sea. Patrice held tight to Greg's hand.

'Nanny?' said Greg as they shuffled down deck.

'Yes dear?'

'I've been thinking.'

'Have you now, you wee dote?'

'Can Auntie Betty see me when I poo?'

Just in front of them, Walkman-yellow-dress girl span around to look at Greg and then up to Patrice, who was momentarily silent as her eyes tennis-balled between the two children. Behind them, Bernard was quietly sniggering towards Nandad, who remained impassive. They moved slowly forward.

'I suppose she must.'

Greg took this in for a moment as they arrived at the gangway and began to trundle down. Bernard and the rest of the family were no longer behind them.

'And can she see you when you poo?'

Patrice shook her head to no-one in particular and continued to shuffle down the narrow gangway.

Greg raised his voice, 'Can Aunty Betty see you when you poo?'

They had reached the end of the gangway now and were slowly spreading out over the concourse. Walkman-yellow-dress girl was still gawping at them as she was dragged away toward a waiting car. Patrice bent down a little and cupped a hand to the side of her mouth.

'Well now Greg, I have to say that I've not given it much thought. But I'm of the opinion that yes, she could. But, Greg, and this is very important, I very much doubt she'd want to see her own mother doing that kind of thing.'

As the crowd thinned Shannon caught up with them and took Greg's hand. She looked at her mother.

'Everything alright, Mum?'

'Oh yes. Just finished a chat with the little man.'

Shannon's eyes moved between the two, but they said nothing more. Nandad and Bernard joined them soon after, their ears now wedged with multiple rollups

'So,' continued Greg, 'Aunty Betty watching us poo is like watching the tele. Like, you can watch ITV or you can watch BBC1. Or you can switch it off and just go to bed.'

'What the fuck is your son on about, Shannon?' mumbled Bernard.

Shannon shifted herself between her brother and child.

'Leave him be, Bernard. He's sensitive.'

Bernard chuckled and rubbed his cheek, 'Yeah, I bet he'll grow up to be real sensitive, Shan. A really sensitive guy.' Bernard sniggered towards Nandad, who remained impassive.

Greg squinted at his uncle for clarity but both women's iced looks demanded Bernard's quick withdrawal. He raised his hands in mock surrender and turned away.

'Don't pay attention to your Uncle,' said Patrice. 'Now listen, look at it this way, ITV or BBC, watching people poo or not watching them poo, it will all be as God intended. So there, that's an end to it now,' and she shoved another wedge of nicotine gum in her gob.

That might have seemed like the end of it but for a fair time after, little Greg was severely constipated. You see, the idea of a ghost you had never met watching you poo was, well, unsettling for Greg. And the idea that God might want the ghosts of dead relatives you had never met watch you poo was also, well, unsettling for Greg. He only got over his constipation by imagining blasting ferry foghorns whilst on the bog. And he does so to this day.

The crowd had now dissipated and the Nacullians were left standing on the concrete, a hundred metres or so from the ferry. They looked about at the alien landscape of the Isle of Wight.

'Mum, what are we going to do now?' asked Greg.

'I told you to stop asking stupid questions. Christ!'

They looked about at the alien landscape of the Isle of Wight.

'When's the ferry back?' asked Bernard.

They looked about at the alien landscape of the Isle of Wight.

Shannon looked at her watch. 'Next one's in an hour.'

Nandad raised a hand. He was pointing at a squat brick building just south of the terminal with a small white sign which read, 'Cowes Café'.

'Let's get some grub,' said Bernard. 'I'm starving since Dad made us miss breakfast.'

'Sounds about right,' said Nandad, who moved off towards the soggy, misted windows of Cowes Café. As if pulled by a thread, the family followed.

Fifteen minutes later, they were all outside the café, armed with floury white baps in white serviettes and steaming Styrofoam mugs. The deep crumbly tang of bacon. The thin bite of granulated coffee. The gulls above, threatening theft and excrement. On a lone picnic table by two green portaloos they ate and drank, in Nacullian silence. Shannon gave Greg his first taste of coffee, which he spat out on the concrete. Bernard sniggered. Nandad remained impassive. By God, it was a beautiful morning.

'Guess we better get in the queue for the ferry back,' said Bernard when they'd finished, 'I hate waiting.'

Soon, the Nacullians were in the queue, complaining about not being able to just get on the damn thing, considering it was just there sitting grey-white on the sea.

Maybe it is like a stone. Maybe it is like vomit. Maybe it is like the head on a pint of rancid ale. Maybe it is like a rabid dog's mouth. Maybe it is only like itself.

When they arrived home, Thunder had pissed everywhere.

CHAPTER THIRTEEN

An Interlude about Water

While this city is by the sea, your average citizen here is sometimes surprised by the fact they live by the sea. This is because being by the sea is something different than being beside the seaside, you see. That's why the city's seaside status is weak in a way, in the kind of way we consider American cheese as cheese or people from Pompey human beings.

Being a seaside place is a whole bundle of ideas people don't usually think about, because people don't usually think. Being by the sea, being truly sea-side, means considering the sea as part of the city. You see, people in seaside places see the sea as part of the city without even thinking about it, because people don't tend to think. For example, when we edge our hot naked little feet into the channel on Bournemouth beach, we aren't escaping Bournemouth, we're embracing it. And drunken July crowds nosediving into the drink off Brighton beach are really drinking in Brighton itself.

In this city though, there's little of the seaside. There's no salt in the air, and the debaucheries of seaside towns are absent. Naturally, there's the common everyday debaucheries of a Luton or a Cwmbran or a Coventry, but that's to be expected. Unlike in a seaside place though, droves of weekenders do not appear in the city on Friday night, with the possible exception of Channel Islanders. And the stag parties and hen parties and office parties and birthday parties are local affairs only, again with the possible exception of Channel Islanders.

It's not that the city doesn't try to make something of its geographical position of being by the sea. The city councillors are forever talking about the sea, and they go about the place promoting the RMS Titanic and the lore surrounding it. This is so that tourists like Kate-or-Rose can come to the city to drink in our chain pubs and shop in our chain stores and eat in our chain restaurants while she runs around finding out about all the Titanicy things the city has to offer.

And another thing the city councillors do is to erect information boards around the old city walls, describing the crumbling crenulations as medieval sea defences against invading continentals. All this though is just a limp marketing trick to make the place seem important and exciting, and no one really falls for it, with the possible exception of Kate-or-Rose and Channel Islanders, of course.

Admittedly, being near the sea has made the city a dockish and a ferryish kind of place and you might even have heard about the odd non-stop heroic swim from Carlingford Loch to the city's docks. Indeed, I'm reliably informed that passenger ships, container ships, tankers, trawlers and tugs do whatever it is they do out there in the Solent, beyond the sea's side. I'm told that the wealth of nations passes through the city and that flags of every nation crowd the sea lanes to the city, but I'm not sure. As a city, you see, we are mostly closed off from the salt.

But just because we are closed off from the salt doesn't mean there's not a good amount to say about the city and the subject of water. Because the city is rich in water, even if it isn't truly by the seaside. The city is thick with water, girded with it. The city is fat with the flow of it and filled with the drip of it. Fresh water, I mean. The city is built around the arms of two rivers. The Test in the west and the Itchen in the east. These are the arms which hold the city up like some bored uncle raising a little brat out of the pool in Bitterne leisure centre.

For example, if you start off from the Nacullian's brick house in the east and head into the city, you cross over Northam Bridge, heading to the centre. There, you'll see some beweeded and sunken hulks sitting in the Itchen's greasy low-tide waters. A historian or marine archaeologist might be able to tell you why they're there, but a school kid travelling on a blue-grey bus in the blue-grey morning might look out at these jutting mud ribs, lit by unseen November sun, and wonder. Now people aren't in the habit of wondering, but water can make you wonder, water can make you think, and people rarely think, rarely wonder, without the aid of water.

Then on the west of the city there's the Test, the broad Test. Moving north, the Test is tousled and bereeded with wetlands, bearded and flexed with tendrils of cool meanders. An ecologist or limnologist might be able to tell you why it's there, but on a muggy July night, you might just dip yourself into the Test and fill up a lung or two with night vapour. Hold it then, hold in that night vapour as you cruise the curve of a marshy meander.

Yes, though the sea isn't part of the city, its rivers certainly are. And another thing about the city and water is that its water is hard, very hard, at least according to maps published by the

125

British Geological Survey. Not that any citizen of the city would notice their hard water though, because people don't tend to notice things. The citizens of this city, the Dunkfords and the Winters and the Nacullians, they just drink tea, they don't need to think about it.

Though no matter how hard the water might be in our area, it's never actually hard, you know, with the possible exception of ice. And it isn't soft either. That's just a hydrological metaphor at play. I state this, because not every quality ascribed to water is metaphorical. For example, it is a little-known fact that most water is damp and only some water, a minority, is wet. To the common uneducated observer, they will of course tell you that water is water is water and that water is certainly wet. But water can have many properties and in the city, it does. And when I call water damp, I'm not talking hydrological metaphor, no. I am far more literal than the British Geological Survey. Water is damp or it's wet dependent on how it's experienced. The meaning of wetness and dampness of water comes down, ultimately, to how we use it.

If you're a little confused, let me explain by examples. Typically, damp water includes drizzle, mists, tears, fogs, snow, sweat, hail, saliva and spray. On occasion, we could include a little spume or a bit of spittle in there too. And typically, your wet water includes river water, lake water, torrential rain, fine rain, bucket water, hose water, sea water, ocean water, flood water. And here on occasion we might include a sprinkle of sprinkler or a dousing of dew.

There's some debate though about whether tap water is damp water or wet water. Well again, it's largely dependent on how it is used. Drink a glass of tap water and sure, that's damp. Throw it over someone like Patrice Nacullian and it'll be wet. Of course, if Patrice Nacullian happens to be on fire, well, that's a different matter altogether, and I'd strongly encourage you to put her out.

This is the principle of water everywhere. The meaning of water is the use of water. It is only ever wet enough for something or damp enough for something or hot enough for this or cool enough for that. And now that you know this, you can understand the city's predicament. To an outsider looking down upon us from a map or a weather report, the city looks like one thing, a city bunched up and bound to the sea. To the historian too, this seems the case and to the city planner, the same again. But if the outsider or the historian or the planner ever comes to the city itself and ever talked to a Dunkford or Winter or a Nacullian, they'd feel the tension between the map and the minutiae. The sea is how we use it and the sea so often seems far away from us here.

The water we know, is fresh.

CHAPTER FOURTEEN

The Second Coming
(1970)

Betty was a boring baby. At least, that's how her father described her.

Since she had been born, Betty had not cried. It was not that she was a mute, it was just that, well, she hadn't got upset yet. She was a quiet baby and a watchful baby. As her parents moved about the little brick house, coming into and out of rooms, coming up and down thinly carpeted stairs, through doorways and down short hallways, she had watched. Sometimes a little burp might have contorted her little face into a smile, but in reality it was just a burp. And sometimes a little yawn might have contorted her little face into a scream, but in reality it was just a yawn.

This quietness and this watchfulness had not gone unnoted by her parents. For himself, Nandad had come to consider Betty to be a baby full of judgement and high scorn. She did not say anything, no, but she judged with her baby eyes and she criticised with her baby noises. She was, he thought, too high and mighty to complain about anything. She went to bed in her cramped little cot without complaint, and always made the pretence of sleeping though the night. She supped up her salty oxosops and her milky milksops without complaint, whether they were warm, or lukewarm or cold. There was even, he thought, a quiet nobility about how she grunted as she filled her nappy, sighing lightly when finished. Queenly. Serene.

'Who does she think she is?' thought Nandad.

And another thing Nandad wasn't fond of was the way she sounded. Betty was nearly sixteen months now and was starting to make something like speech, but it was a weird speech. It was a speech bent and accented with the sounds of the Upper Bann and the border counties thereabouts:

'Gung,' she would say.

'Hoow,' she would intone.

'Oose,' she would coo.

'Naaa,' she would state.

But they were not around the Upper Bann or the border counties thereabouts. This child was an English child, but she spoke a gibberish like home, and Nandad did not like it. Was she mocking him maybe? Was this watchful and judgemental and uncomplaining baby simply ripping the shite out of her poor Da with her sounds of the Upper Bann and the border counties thereabouts?

And so, 'who does she think she is?' thought Nandad. Though Nandad quietly noted to himself that having an inferiority complex with a baby was a wee bit childish on his part, so he decided that she was boring instead. It was true that when it came to his child, there was an anger about the fact there was precious little to be angry about, and thinking about his anger at this lack of cause for anger made him angrier still.

For Patrice, the matter was different. After she had given birth, she had been ill. Whenever Betty was passed to her, the baby seemed almost too cold and too heavy to hold, though she was told her daughter was underweight and had been running a fever. And her milk was slow to come too, a creeping stream from her breasts, and the nurses told her that this would not do, that she must try harder. She was a mother now, they said. And Patrice did try harder, she let the heavy, cold thing pull her raw nipples into its mouth, but what little she could produce felt like a bowel-deep draining of her, and soon her breasts were put out to pasture.

But despite the weakness she felt in herself, somehow not long after, she had become pregnant. And now, eight months later she had been advised rest, counselled rest, demanded rest. Though still in her, never having left her, was this bloodless feeling, this sapped and snapped supine and sallow feeling. She looked down at her own swollen self and marvelled at how her body had allowed her to become pregnant once more. Though she didn't want to admit it, she felt that maybe her body was already too old for this, that her twenties were gone now and all this pregnancy stuff was a kind of disease she was losing the fight to.

What this meant was that for much of Betty's early life, Patrice was often too sick and sapped to form much of an opinion of her first daughter. But thankfully, Betty was such a quiet child, such an abiding baby, that no opinion was necessary. It was such a relief to have so little trouble with this one. Heavily pregnant as she was now, Patrice tried to distract herself from her pains and her pangs and her twinges and aches by completing books of crossword puzzles and by working through packets of long, strong cigarettes. Her brain was full of words and her lungs were full of smoke and her womb was full of baby. And with all this fullness, there was little room left for anything else.

In the daytime, if Nandad was out on the building sites, Patrice would be sat up in bed, with Betty placed below her on a thin particoloured mat. The child was given a few things and some stuff to keep her occupied and she played and sucked and crawled and stared about without complaint. A quiet baby. An abiding baby. This meant that Patrice would only have to be out of bed a few times a day to make breakfast, lunch and dinner. Betty would sleep with her in the afternoons and sometimes play on the bed, though Patrice was always frightened that her daughter might fall off. In some of her daydreams, she imagined her husband coming home and walking into the room to see his wife buckled over in lament while a bent-necked child, cold and heavy, lay on the floor below her.

And with a voice emanating as though through water, he would say, 'And what is it ye did this time?'

Sometimes she thought her daydreams seemed like her nightdreams, and she found them hard to escape, hard to pull herself out of and back to her room.

As for the most part Patrice was unable to go outside, she relied on giving Nandad a list of things and stuff to buy on his way back from work. And once or twice she had called on the services of Mary Clemens next door, who occasionally popped round to check on her. Whenever she did, Patrice got her to pick up a bar of dripping or a loaf of bread or a half-pound of tea when she was up at the grocer's.

Mary had mentioned a couple of times now that couldn't they maybe write home and get some help over? They must be from a large family, surely? Surely Patrice had a few sisters, surely? Maybe the husband had a niece who needed somewhere to stay? Patrice nodded at these things and said that yes, maybe they could get someone over. But when Mary left, so did the suggestion.

'She's a boring wee thing,' Nandad said a few weeks later, as Betty tottered quietly around the Nacullian's living room. It was a Sunday morning and Nandad was sitting in his new green armchair, a paper covering his face and the crackle of a valve radio warming a frigid atmosphere.

Patrice was standing up stirring a mug of tea, as she looked abstractly at a painting above the fireplace. It was of a man drawing a draft horse through a muddy field, somewhere around the Upper Bann or the border counties thereabouts. She remembered it had been sent to them, over ten years ago now. His brother. A condolence disguised as a gift.

'I say, Pat, she's a boring wee thing.'

Her legs felt weak.

'Hoow,' Betty intoned.

'Pat?'

Her bowels ached.

'Naaa,' Betty stated.

'Pat!'

Nandad took her by the shoulder roughly enough that a blob of tea left the cup and plopped on to the brown living room carpet.

'I'm sorry, I don't know where I was, love,' she said to Nandad, looking at him abstractly, as though through him.

'You need to be in bed,' he said.

'I need to be in bed,' she said.

Nandad picked up Betty and followed Patrice up the stairs to their room. He plopped his daughter on the particoloured mat and pulled the bedcovers over his wife. Once she had lit a cigarette and had opened her crossword book, Patrice seemed much better and Nandad went back downstairs.

Below her, Betty played with things and stuff. Such a quiet child. Such an abiding baby. Never cries. She sleeps through the night too. Such a relief, such a relief to have so little trouble with this one.

Five across: A structure used to separate different areas. Four letters.

Patrice pondered. She tapped some ash into a green ashtray on the bedside table. She took a long, crisp drag on her cigarette.

'Gung,' said Betty.

'Ah,' Patrice said, and wrote.

Nine down: Kind of mud brick. Five letters, beginning 'a'.

Patrice pondered. She tapped some ash into a green ashtray on the bedside table. She took short puff on her cigarette.

'Oose,' cooed Betty.

'Ah,' Patrice said, and wrote.

Twenty-six down: The idea that nothing is planned in advance. Five letters, fourth letter 'o'.

Patrice pondered. She stubbed her fag out into a green ashtray on the bedside table.

Betty said nothing. She was filling her nappy in a queenly and serene way.

A quarter of an hour later, the crossword was full of blue ballpoint letters. Thunder was a sound made during a storm, the Nile was the longest river in Egypt and suicide was an action bound to end in failure. Almost done. Almost there. Twenty-six down though still had Patrice stumped. The five letter word with its fourth letter 'o' drooped off near the edge of the page like a damp cigarette.

'Five letters, with an 'o',' she muttered. 'The idea that nothing is planned in advance.'

Patrice's bowels ached.

'Hoow,' intoned Betty, who had got up from her particoloured mat and was clunkily cruising her way down toward the bottom of the bed.

Almost done. Almost there. Patrice sucked on the end of her ballpoint pen.

Downstairs, some kind of DIY was taking place and the radio was still on. Though Patrice didn't know it, Simon and Garfunkel were playing:

> ♪ (...) you're (...) (...) out ♫
> ♫ When (...) on the street ♪
> ♪ When evening (...) so hard ♫
> ♫ (...) will comfort you (ooo) ♪

'Ah!' said Patrice.

'Naaa,' stated Betty, as she dribbled on to her parents' floral bedspread.

'Ah!' said Patrice, louder this time, and wrote.

Chaos is the idea that nothing is planned in advance.

Nandad could be heard coming up the stairs. He was humming Simon and Garfunkel. Still clinging to the bedspread, Betty looked toward the doorway as Nandad entered. Betty contorted her little face into what looked like a smile, which was in reality a smile. Her first.

Nandad had a clawhammer in his hand and was looking at Patrice, 'And what did ye do this time?' he said.

Patrice startled at the sound and glared abstractly in its direction, as if looking through water. 'Ah!' she shouted.

'For dinner I mean,' said Nandad, 'What have ye done for the dinner?'

Patrice gasped, a cold heavy gasp that drew a wide-eyed look from Betty.

'Almost done. Almost there,' she said.

The blue ballpoint pen dropped from her hand. The covers of the bed were warm and wet like milksops.

Predestination is the idea that all is planned in advance.

They had no other option but to leave Betty with Mary and Cliff Clemens next door. Betty's little face contorted into a scream, which was in reality a scream. Her first.

CHAPTER FIFTEEN

Hot to Cold
(c.1954)

They say no one can see the future. You can have your expectations and your hopes and you can have your flutters on this dog or on that horse. But no one can actually see the future. The IMF and Nostradamus and Zoltar the Magnificent are, ultimately, all in the same boat.

But while we can't see into the future, we think we can see into the past. The past we think, is easier to see. We have the photos and the videos and documents to prove it, after all. The past is easier to see than the future we think, because the past has happened already. We think that the past is just sitting there, waiting for us.

I'll admit that while I think very highly of myself as a narrator, the past isn't always clear to me. The past can be difficult to see, especially when things are very old or when they are nearly forgotten. Now, if you asked me what Greg Nacullian had for breakfast on the morning of his eighteenth birthday in 2004, I'd tell you straight off that he had rice puffs with semi-skimmed milk and two extra spoons of sugar. And if you asked me for the colour of Shannon's eyes, I'd tell you without flinching that they were a pale, pale blue.

But there are gaps. Sometimes the past feels to me like a system of roadways. It's easy to go certain places, but sometimes you encounter the toll bridge over by Woolston, or heavy traffic on Shirley High Street and sometimes you're pushing a stolen moped up a gravel track through the woods at the back of Thornhill. It's dark there and it's wet there and you're stumbling. And you're only pushing the moped into the woods because you're going to set the shitty thing on fire, and you're not even sure why. It's this kind of past that's hard to remember.

What is about to come involves a past I'm not altogether sure about, because sometimes there are more gaps than there is anything else, and trying to remember is like pushing that moped up a darkened gravel track, when it's wet and you're stumbling.

16 years old when it happened. A long time ago. Born quickly and died quickly. A lung problem, a small thing. He was a small thing. Named after her father. Niall. Her own father never saw though. Just as well.

Because a man once. In a hedge once. Down the nameless road. Near St Mochta's House. Into the hedge, cut this way and that by bramble. Asked for everything and she gave everything. Amazing things fear can do. Not of age she told him, but with a dripping wee thing like that he says, you are, you bloody are. And yes, she knew him. Known to her family. But the name forgotten now. Just as well.

It could happen, then. To her. To a good girl like her, as she used to think of herself. Not being unlucky, no. Not being whorish, no. But the world being the way the world was. Could happen to anyone. But that was that.

But that wasn't that. It starts coming on. Baby starts coming on and this has consequences. You can't stay where you're at. When baby starts coming on you can't stay where you're at. Get away or you're sent away.

Then another man comes. From over the border. No one special. A little older. A quick proposal. Does he know what he's getting? Damn right he knows what he's getting. Desperate himself. Took her on when women needed taking on. And husband now. She's grateful now. Amazing things fear can do. Honeymoon picnic at Carlingford.

And to England, to the city. Just 16. It's fast coming on now. Barely settled. No picnic. In the hospital now. A grunt. A whimper. Her whimper. A heave now. A push now. A tut. Try harder. Push harder.

The husband above her. The rafters. The matron. The funny gas. A suck now. That's better. Try harder. Heave harder. Some sweat. Some water. Her waters. They talk. They whisper. The husband above her.

They nod now. The funny gas. More funny gas. Now heave now. Heave-ho now. Those rafters. That funny gas. The matron. That matron. That tutting. Tut-tut. Tut-tutting.

The thing now. Below her. Through numbness. Still feel it. Can sense it. A squirm there. A fidget. Below her. Can't see it. So push now. Breathe push now. It's there now? Not quite now. A suck now. Not long now.

The husband. Hand holder. More water. Cool water. The forehead. The sweating. They whisper. The nurses. A grunt there. Grunt harder. A curse there. They whisper.

Hold on now. Hand holder. Last push now. A scream there. That's better. That's good there. A whimper. A fidget. A squirm there. Through numbness. They nod now. The nurses. The husband. That's better.

A hot thing. Below her. Can sense him. A small thing. A warm thing. The blanket. That's better. It's cold here. The matron. She whispers. To husband. They nod then. Slow nod then. Enough now. Nurse takes him.

A curse then. Enough now. Hand holder. Hold harder. Calm down there. Curse harder. A tut. Tut-tutting. Clean up there, hereafter. Drink water. Cold water. Relax now, they simper. The nurses. They simper. It's cold here. Through numbness. A blanket. The rafters. It's cold here. Can feel it. It's cold here, hereafter.

Hold on now, they whisper. No more push now. No more heave. No more grunt and no curse. No matron or nurses. Just husband, hand holder. No spasm or fidget. No screaming or whimper. Warm now. No matron. The rafters. Those rafters.

Then matron. Then nodding. A tut. Tut-tutting. Hold husband, hold harder. The matron. Her hands there. Her hands there, they're empty. Can't see it. Can't sense it. Can't calm down. Can't clean up. Can't hold it. Hands empty. Through numbness. All over.

The husband above her. A lung problem. A small thing. He, was a small thing. Niall. Asked his name. For the certificates. Birth and death. No sound. No scream. No curse. Then her father's name. Niall.

Amazing things fear can do.

Like I say, the past isn't always clear to me and it's true that sometimes, we have neither the photos or the videos or the documents to prove it. You can have your suspicions and your reconstructions and you can have your educated guess about this scrap of information or that piece of gossip. But no one can actually see the past, because the past isn't just sitting there, waiting for us. If you asked me what Patrice Nacullian had for breakfast on the morning of her sixteenth birthday in 1954, I could only guess that it would be a piece of bread and jam with a mug of tea. And if you asked me for the colour of Niall's eyes, I simply couldn't tell you.

CHAPTER SIXTEEN

A Lesson in History
(1997)

Adults teach children history to show them this folly or that injustice, or this cruelty or that stupidity. It's all famine this and beheading that, all firebombs this and invasions that. Adults think if children know about the famines and the firebombs, then they won't repeat them. And this is what gets me, the fact that adults demand that their children live their lives in less of a foolish fucking stupidly cruel way than theirs have been lived. If you want to know my opinion, that's the worst kind of sloppy optimism. And if you want to know something about history, it's that the sloppy optimists always get shot first, much to the relief of everybody else.

And by lucky coincidence, history was just one of the many edifying subjects taught as part of the National Curriculum at Dumbledown Junior School. If you want to know something of its history, then it opened in 1969, and that's about all the history you need to know. Well, that's not strictly true. There's something else worth mentioning too. Dumbledown Junior was the Nacullian's school, and had taught two generations, beginning with Betty, Shannon, Bernard and then Greg.

I could have told you something about any of these Nacullians and their time in Dumbledown. There's the one about Betty winning a Hampshire-wide school poetry competition in 1979 for her poem 'Here comes the twenty-first century'. The poem has since been lost, otherwise I would have reprinted it here for you. And then there's Shannon's year 4 school report where her teacher, Mrs Frank, wrote to Nandad and Patrice telling them their daughter was an unpromising retard. Shannon's campaign of truancy started soon after. The report has since been ripped up, otherwise I would have reprinted it here. And of course there's the time Bernard found a scrap of pornography in Thornhill Park woods and used the school photocopier to sell tit-and-stocking reproductions in the playground for 20p a pop. He turned a tidy profit. The scrap of pornography has since been lost, otherwise I would have reprinted it here. This scrap of novel though is about Greg, if for no other reason than that the materials haven't been lost, and can be reprinted here for the first time, truthfully and faithfully.

Dumbledown Junior was a school of flat concrete playgrounds and sloped muddy playing fields that did not distinguish itself in any way whatsoever bar one, which was that all its teachers had strangely appropriate names. For example:

Ms Shard was very sharp.

Mr McCurry was hotheaded.

Mrs Salisbury was from Salisbury.

Mr Cargo was a supply teacher.

Mrs Poll was the head.

Mrs May was born in May.

Mrs Winter was always cold.

And so on and so forth. Exam results at the school were

unremarkably below average, and a government inspector found Dumbledown Junior to be the most unexciting kind of mediocre, where both excellence and disaster were somehow utterly beyond its reach. The only time Dumbledown got into the papers was in 1990 with an article in the Daily Echo about a Mr Fiddler, who'd left the school in suspicious circumstances. And that really is about it.

But while generally unremarkable, the children of Dumbledown were very much alive to the peculiarity in the naming of staff, and they collectively saw it as their duty to maintain a relation between the name of a teacher and their life in the school. Any new teachers were expected to conform to the Dumbledown rule. If they could not or would not, then they were usually driven out by a mixture of bad behaviour and low-level collegial bullying.

One teacher for example was Ms Wednesday, who had the misfortune of not being born on a Wednesday. More than this though, when asked by the children of 3A on what day she was born, the answer she gave did not include the word Wednesday. Incensed by this lack of connection, the children of class 3A decided they could only solve the tension by listening to Ms Wednesday on a Wednesday. On any day that was not a Wednesday, they would pretend she was invisible and run about the class singing a song they had communally composed called, 'Where's our Teacher?' It went something like this:

> ♪ Can't find the teacher ♫
> ♫ Go and tell the head ♪
> ♪ The teacher works on Wednesdays ♫
> ♫ On other days she's dead! ♪

And so on and so forth.

'You could have just told the class you were born on a Wednesday, Ms Wednesday, and they wouldn't have given you one-half of all this terrible trouble,' said Mrs Poll, as she sat opposite the wet-faced and crumpled figure of her newest teacher.

'But, but, M-Mrs P-Poll' stammered Ms Wednesday through tears, 'I wasn't born on a Wednesday. I was born on a Tuesday morning!'

'Well, that's close enough, isn't it?'

'Mrs Poll, are you suggesting that I lie to the children?'

Mrs Poll though had no opportunity to answer this question as Ms Wednesday streamed from the office, never to return. Mrs Poll shook her head and flicked through the black leather Filofax on her desk. After a moment, she fingered a page with her lilac nail and picked up the phone.

'Hello. Is that Cargo? Good. Yes, you are needed for class 3A. As soon as possible please, Mr Cargo. Yes. I shall occupy them with eye-spy in the meantime.'

In keeping with its reputation for unremarkability, Dumbledown Junior School dinners were neither famous nor infamous. They edged, side-on and gut tucked in, between the two narrowly separated chairs of palatability and government regulation, managing to just about avoid both. The canteen manager Mrs Cook had a small team of part-time dinner ladies, who for the sake of safety were all told to assume the name Mrs Chips when

144

around the children.

Mrs Cook had a simple and effective philosophy when it came to food, which was that children would generally be happy with food which was either yellow or beige. Brown was also acceptable. But anything outside this palette of safety was to be avoided on the grounds that green or red food was expensive and always went uneaten. Better a child full of brown and yellow and beige, thought Mrs Cook, than an empty child with a lot of green and red leftovers.

Greg Nacullian was a half-empty child who was currently working on a half-full plate of warm-beige-and-yellowbrown-globlets. He was sitting in the middle of a long laminated table in the half-empty canteen, as screams and whoops from the half-full playground echoed around the hall. As he folded warm beige food into tepid yellowbrown food, he was moderately deep in thought.

That Friday morning, Greg's teacher Mrs Brewer had called in sick again, and Mr Cargo was brought in to teach class 6C. Being a familiar enough presence in Dumbledown, Mr Cargo was under the false impression he was liked and respected by the children. In reality though, he was only tolerated because his name related in some way to how the children saw him.

'Hello there Class 6C. It is I, Mr Cargo, again.'

'Hello Mr Cargo,' the class intoned.

'Mrs Brewer is ill again today, Class 6C.'

'Ahhhh,' the class let out a pantomime sigh, which gave Mr Cargo the false impression they were sensitive children.

Once these formalities were over and with Mrs Poll staring through the classroom door's little window, Mr Cargo thought it best to begin teaching. Now, because he was a supply teacher and didn't know what he was doing, Mr Cargo told the class they had to write stories.

Too loudly and with eyes darting toward the little window, Mr Cargo said, 'Today Class 6C, we will write some stories. This will improve your grammar and comprehension.'

Through the little window, he could see Mrs Poll give a firm nod, before she disappeared from view. He heard the click of heels fading down the hallway and inwardly, Mr Cargo sighed.

'What should we write stories about, Mr Cargo?' asked Lily Baker, without raising her hand.

Now because Mr Cargo didn't really know what he was doing and because he didn't know anything about stories, he said the children should use their imagination and write whatever they wanted to. But then, because he didn't want to look like he was making things up on the spot, he qualified this by telling the children that under no circumstances could they draw pictures to go along with their stories. Stories were stories, he said, and pictures were pictures. He repeated. Stories are stories, pictures are pictures.

'Yes,' he thought to himself, 'That sounds like Mr Cargo knows what he is doing.'

Mr Cargo clapped his hands to commence the activity, and then as the children got underway, he edged himself around to sit behind Mrs Brewer's desk. The children were writing furiously and the quiet clink of glass sounded as Mr Cargo went through Mrs Brewer's drawers.

Sitting next to Lily Baker, Greg Nacullian was in his usual place, a hexagon made of two tables in the middle of the classroom. He wrote this story, which as I said before, thankfully hasn't been lost.

*The Story of How the Nickelodeon Family Saved the World
and made Bitterne Lezure Centre
By Greg Nacullian
Class 6C*

This is about people who live in a house made of brick. The Nickelodeon family were a family. They lived in a big brick house made of brick. They lived in a big brick house in a southern city. In the southern city they lived in the east. The east part of the city. Three lots of the Nickelodeon family lived in the brick house, which was really good because people don't normally like one another very much. They lived in wonderful harmony. The Nanny and Nandad of the family were from somewhere else. They came to the city because their home was oreful and beautiful. When Nanny Nickelodeon came she magically made food for all the starving children to eat. When Nandad Nickelodeon come he magically made Bitterne Lezure Centres everywhere all over the world, so that the children could go swimming and go on the floom. Then Nandad Nickelodeon died because he was so tired of building Bitterne Lezure Centres everywhere. Then there was only Nanny Nickelodeon left to feed all the children. The rest of the family was also magical and did amazing things and saved the world but it is lunch break now.

With the bell ringing and with inward relief, Mr Cargo opened the door to let Class 6C out.

One thing that I haven't yet mentioned was that Greg was convinced Mr Cargo was his father. For some time now Greg had been wondering, and so far Mr Cargo seemed the most likely candidate. Mr Cargo's large beard and large glasses were the perfect disguise, thought Greg, for his father to come in and visit him. And the role of a supply teacher was the perfect job, wasn't it, to pop in now and then to check on his son. And the fact Mr Cargo really didn't seem to know what he was doing was also evidence that Mr Cargo was not really a teacher but was in fact Greg's father.

Greg though sometimes had his doubts about this theory and sometimes these doubts interfered with his project on life in Roman Britain or with the futuristic pictures of the twenty-first century he was asked to draw by Mrs Brewer. His doubts went something like this. Why would his dad need a disguise, if Greg didn't know what he looked like in the first place? And why would Mr Cargo tell him off at break for beating up Dave Kerins from 5B, when dads liked it when their sons beat up other kids? And why did Mr Cargo tell him to stop talking stupid nonsense when he asked him if he was really his dad in disguise? These were puzzlements indeed, and difficult for Greg's eleven-year-old brain to balance.

All these doubts were hardly surprising, because there was a fuzzy lump in Greg's life. He did not know the shape or the colour or the extent of it, but it was there and it had the name of father. Greg knew too that even though it was there, it could not, under any circumstances, be talked about. The subject was untouchable, like salad in a school canteen. The one time he had asked his Nan where he came from, she only told him that he was a gift, a gift which God had intended. Then she said something about the Virgin Mary being given a gift, so who were we to question such things? The world was, after all, the world, wasn't it?

Greg's suspicion about Mr Cargo then was about as good a theory as any. But there was a need to get some kind of confirmation from him, some nod or suggestion or something, anything. For whatever reason, Greg's loving and devoted father could not reach out to his boy, was prevented somehow, held back somehow. This was the fuzzy lump's fault, but Greg didn't know why.

The class returned after second break and were sitting on the little octagonal islands of learning spread around the class. Mr Cargo cleared his throat to speak, because that was what he thought real teachers did.

'Class 6C,' said Mr Cargo, 'Mrs Poll, your headmistress, has told me you are learning about the Romans. Now, is this true?'

'Yes, Mr Cargo,' replied Class 6C.

'And is it also true that you are making very exciting projects about these Romans?' said Mr Cargo.

'Yes, Mr Cargo,' replied Class 6C.

'I see. I see. And what is it that you would like to tell me about these Romans?'

A bubble of twisting hands rose up, higher, higher, competing with their foes for attention. Mr Cargo scanned the room and waited.

'The Romans ate fishgut sauce!' shouted Holly Smith.

'Latin!' called out Johnny Radley.

'The Romans were from Rome!' bellowed Lizzie Kostek.

'Veni, video, Fiji!' sang Manu Alsaid.

'The Romans were Christians!' screamed Robert Mason.

'The Romans killed Christians!' retorted Candy Dunkford.

'Carpe die!' trilled Chris Winter.

'The Romans invaded Britain!' exclaimed Aaron Stretcher.

'The Romans abandoned Britain!' argued Kerry Header.

'Percussa Brickim!' cried Greg Nacullian.

Mr Cargo looked around at Class 6C with satisfaction, for he saw what a wonderful thing being a primary school supply teacher was. There was no kind of school day that couldn't be fully supplied by asking the children to write stories and then asking them what they knew about something or other. As long as he called writing stories 'an exercise to improve grammar and comprehension' and as long as he labelled asking them what their real teacher had been teaching them as 'checking knowledge', Mr Cargo was in the clear. A long and calm and comfortable life of stories without pictures stretched out before him.

The class continued on with their scraps and photocopies of Roman facts and phrases.

'And so on and so forth,' thought Mr Cargo, 'And so on and so forth.'

The bell had rung the end of the school day and the rest of 6C had left. Greg though had hung back and was pretending he was unable to fit his pencils into his pencil case. Seeing the child worried Mr Cargo, as he remembered Greg was the one who for a week in year 4 had followed him around asking strange questions about dads and fathers and daddies.

'Mr Cargo?'

With pencils now put away, Greg was now slowly putting the pencil case into his satchel.

'What it is, Gregory Nacullian?'

Greg closed up his satchel with a click. 'Is Mr Cargo your real name?'

'I don't know what you mean. What do you mean, Gregory Nacullian?'

'Like, do you have another name outside school?' He looped the satchel strap over his shoulder.

'Outside of school is outside of school, Gregory. That is Mr Cargo's private business.'

'Yeah, like, I know it is. But...'

'Come now, Gregory. It is after school already and Mr Cargo needs to be going home.'

'But, like, like, what do your own children call you?'

A pause. Mr Cargo looked one way down the hallway, then the other way. He thumbed his knuckle into his beard, pushing the wiry hair into the skin of his neck. What did this child want of him? Was this a government inspection trap? What did Mr Cargo have to say so that Mr Cargo could go home and have his long and calm and comfortable weekend of stories without pictures?

'I will answer your question, Gregory, if you promise to go home right after.'

Greg took a little step towards the supply teacher. Mr Cargo nodded at him.

'You see, Gregory,' said Mr Cargo, 'the truth of the matter is that all my children call me Mr Cargo.'

Another pause. The corridor quiet. The child quiet. The beard soft against his neck. The child staring at him.

'I'll call you Mr Cargo then,' said Greg finally, and he made his way through the classroom door and into the quiet corridor.

The next time Mrs Poll called him up, Mr Cargo said that

sadly, his services had just been called upon elsewhere in the city. He said the same thing the next time she called too. Eventually, they found another supply teacher called Mrs Weakday, and everyone was happy enough with her services, especially because she knew something about Roman history.

CHAPTER SEVENTEEN

Neighbours from Nowhere
(1998)

'So I'm in the old club the other day and I goes to visit the gents. Before I go in though, I look at the little man on the door, you know, the little man that tells you the gents is the gents. I look at him and see these little bumps on the fella, like he's got measles downstairs or something. I reach up and touch 'em, the bumps, and they're raised, really raised, like. And then it hits me: It's blind-writing, innit?

'So fair enough I think, mystery solved, and then I goes in. And I'm standing there and I'm thinking about this little man with the blind-writing written on him. But then I'm like hold on, how's any blind guy going to find this blind-writing in the first place? A few little dots in the middle of a door is all it is. What, is he meant to go round, feeling any and every surface in the hope he'll find the word Men, or whatever men is in the blind-language? He'd have pissed himself by then, poor sod.

'Then I start to notice that the blind-writing isn't only on the bloody doors of the bogs, but it's all over the shop. The welcome sign's got it, the club secretary's office's got it, even the bloody cleaning cupboard's got it. I'm up and down the club now as I'm gonna bloody well find out how much of this stuff there is in the place. The answer. A lot of it. And I'll be buggered if any blind bugger's going to be reading them signs anytime soon.

'So it's all bloody useless, these dots. Worse than useless. Like, I'd understand if it was in a book. You'd pass the book over to the blind fella and he's away, reading whatever his blind heart desires. Nothing against him. Good on him, I say. Good luck to him. But why put blind-writing in a place no blind bugger'll be able to find it? So, it's all bloody useless. Worse than useless.

'So anyway, that's what I was thinking last night.'

Cliff gave a sniff. He had his elbows rested on the top of the panel fence and his hairless white arms were waxy in the bright light. Below him, Patrice Nacullian was looking into her half-empty teacup.

'Well Cliff,' said Patrice, still staring into her tea, 'if God wants there to be braille on the cleaning cupboard of Thornhill working men's club then there'll be braille on the cleaning cupboard of Thornhill working men's club.'

Cliff gave several short snorts, like he had heard and agreed with what Patrice had said. Then he nodded as he always did after his little speeches and disappeared back down into his own garden. Maybe it was because it was a hot day and there really was nothing much to do, but Cliff waited against the fence, listening. He could hear Patrice still in the same spot, could hear the faint clinks of her spoon against her cup. Eventually, after a minute maybe, he heard the shuffle of movement and soon after a door opened, closed.

It was only after Old Man Nacullian had died last year that Cliff had decided to up his level of neighbourliness to the Nacullians. Patrice was a lovely woman and he worried about her.

He had always liked the Nacullians with that abstract kind of like we reserve for greengrocers and milkmen and bus drivers on our local route. The Nacullians had always kept their back garden neat and tidy and had never let the buddleia take over. For Cliff that was evidence enough that the family was in good moral order. For a garden was never just a garden.

The Nacullian's back garden started with a little concrete strip, outside a glass-panelled door, that ran the length of the house. The strip was linked at one end to a set of concrete steps that led up to the garden proper, with its modest lawn. Most of the garden was fringed with hedges of privet and beech and near the centre, a little slab-lined pond stood watch, accompanied by a simple wooden bird feeder. At the back, linked by a pebbly path to the concrete stairs, was Old Man Nacullian's shed, a thin, high shed, tanned by creosote and bleached by sun.

But since Old Man Nacullian had gone into the ground, Cliff had become increasingly concerned for Patrice, for her loneliness, what must have been her loneliness, and for her garden too, lest it should slip from being ship-shape and fall into bad order without her husband there to help her. To alleviate this fear of his and of course to alleviate her own loneliness, Cliff had made it his business to talk to her whenever possible and about anything he could think of. He shared with her all his thoughts on family, on community, on politics, the weather, gardening, social events and festivities, the weather, hobbies, the weather, on religion, the seasons, the weather, and of course on Thornhill working men's club's provisions for the visually impaired.

For himself, Cliff was a founding member of the Clemens family, who had been the Nacullian's neighbours since, oh, the late sixties at least. Both of his children had left years ago and it was just him and his Mary now. He used to drive buses all around the city and thereabouts, as far as Totton in the west and West End in the east. But he had packed that in a while ago and it was just him and his Mary now.

To most people associated with Cliff it was unclear if his Mary had left him, was dead, or was some sort of housebound cripple, because she was never seen and was only remembered as a blur that every Thursday used to purchase a saveloy and small chips from Chippy Chips down the road. But no one asked him about his Mary. No one asked Cliff much of anything in fact. Probably because Cliff was a bland, boring, sad man altogether, the kind of man you could only like in that abstract kind of way we like greengrocers and milkmen and bus drivers on our local route. And when bus drivers stop being bus drivers, well, they slip away from us, silently.

Patrice was staring into the pond, at what, Cliff could not see. But it seemed a long stare. A hard stare. She was so still that the sparrows were feeding from the bird table next to her.

'Hello there, Patrice.'

'Morning Cliff.'

'Out in the garden again?'

'I'm out in the garden again.'

'Spring's here.'

'Spring is here.'

'No April showers.'

'No. No April showers, Cliff.'

'I suppose you've heard the news.'

'I'm no news buff these days, now Cliff.'

'Well, your lot have sorted themselves out.'

'How's that now?' Patrice remained fixed on the depths of the pond. The sparrows had abated and were chirp-chirping from inside the buddleia near the back of the garden.

'Heard it on the news. Finally signed it off. Saw Tony and the Irish whatsamecallit and then that Trimble bloke and the terrorists. Looks like all the nonsense is done with.'

'Is that so?'

'It's all over the news. Headlines everywhere. Worldwide they say.'

'Is that so?'

'So that's good news.'

'Sure, that's good news. But I'm no news buff nowadays, Cliff.'

'Well, I thought you'd want to know,' said Cliff, 'that your lot have sorted themselves out.'

'Well thanks for letting me know that, Cliff.'

'You're welcome, Patrice, you're welcome,' and with this he gave an uncharacteristic thumbs up, arm straight out, like an ecstatic American. And then, realising he didn't really feel like an American and he didn't feel ecstatic, he retracted his arm and slid back down into his own garden, with a nod of goodbye.

From his own garden, Cliff listened. Listened for Patrice. For what she was thinking. What she was feeling. While all the family used the garden Cliff would only really pop up when Patrice was there and he preferred catching her on her own whenever possible. From his position behind the fence he had trained himself to tune into each of them, to become accustomed to their little habits.

Shannon was easy to listen out for, because she was a curser and when in the garden she would curse Godssake fuckssake Christsake as she moved about, as if somehow everything was always slightly out of place. The son Bernard hardly went into the garden, but when he did he was guaranteed to lurch his way along the pebbly path up to his father's shed. He would close the door quietly and remain in there, not making any sound, for a good long while. And then after a good long while, he'd come back out, the shed door closed quietly behind him, and from there directly back into the house. Shannon's boy was another easy one, as he generally came out to play basketball, for which the garden was very badly designed. The slap slap of his underinflated ball along the concrete strip was sign enough that Cliff shouldn't be using up his neighbourliness just yet.

Sometimes he brought his Mary into the garden, but only when he knew the Nacullians were out. Though he knew it was silly, he didn't want them to see his Mary and perhaps more than this, he didn't want his Mary to see the Nacullians. His life in the house and his life in the garden were two separate things, and the Nacullians were part of garden life, his garden life. His Mary was house life, and down-the-shops life. Sometimes though Cliff would drive her to Victoria Country Park and they would eat bacon sandwiches outside the wood panelled café there. They would look down at the old hospital chapel on the green and Cliff would pass comment on the weather, or the tea, or the thickness of the bacon or the greenness of the green, or on the weather.

Cliff heard the click of the Nacullian's back door as Patrice went back in. He was worried about her. About her loneliness now without her husband beside her, though true, he never really got to know Old Man Nacullian. He was never very talkative was Old Man Nacullian. Whenever Cliff tried to get a conversation going about the weather or bus driving or gardening or how the kids were doing or the weather, he'd get a forced smile and a few words. The man seemed short on words most of the time, though Cliff reflected that there were quite a few people he tried to talk to who didn't seem interested. In fact, by and large, the world didn't seem particularly interested.

The only real exception, he had always felt, had been Patrice. She'd always have a few spots of time for a chat or a natter, about this or about that. They even had a proper talk once, something about a Saint she liked. St Mocha? St Mohawk? No, but something like that. But a proper talk it was. She was a lovely woman, Cliff had always told his Mary. She was a lovely woman.

That was until her Old Man had died. Cliff never got the impression they liked one another much, and he remembered a couple of nights when the sounds coming through the wall suggested there was very little fondness. That was a long time ago, though. But when her Old Man died there was a shift in Patrice. Before, when he'd occasionally chat to her over the fence, Patrice would chuckle and shake her head and look right at him with her small, pale eyes. But now she seemed, well not sad, but just, to herself, in herself.

And he was making a real effort, was Cliff, with the neighbourliness. Because, well, because he thought she must be lonely. And she was a lovely woman. And they were neighbours. And what were neighbours for, after all? Once or twice he had even sat quiet on the log under the fence for an hour or more waiting to see if she might come out to dig a few bulbs or sit out for a bit of sun. But after Old Man Nacullian had gone his way, she came out less and she spoke less and sometimes, just sometimes, Cliff might have described her as being maybe just a little rude.

In his bed, Cliff was dreaming. On the other side of the room the form of his Mary rose and fell in the relative darkness. Her respirator whirred in the relative darkness, too. Cliff though did not see his Mary nor hear the whirr of her respirator, because he was dreaming. He was dreaming of Patrice Nacullian.

In his dream he was stood up on his log, his white arms resting on the top of the Clemens-Nacullian fence. He was looking over into the Nacullian's garden, and it was silent. It was strange how even though no one was in the garden it was the lack of Patrice that he noticed. The absence of Patrice was there, was real, whereas the absence of Shannon's boy, or Shannon or the Australian Prime Minister or an empty pint of milk or anything else, was neither here nor there. The garden was absent of Patrice only.

The garden was serene, from his position on the top of the fence. The pond was still, the grass verdant and the buddleia in the far corner had been trimmed back to keep in line with a heavy hedge of privet and beech. The bird table was full of seed and the shed had just been given a coat of creosote, which tanged the still air. There was no birdsong, nor the rumble of roads or the shouts of children. Cliff stood watching the creosote-tinged stillness of the garden for some time, as the absence of Patrice dripped into him. He kept looking toward the Nacullian's backdoor with its large glass panel, watching for movement in the kitchen. Though there was no movement.

But from the little slab-lined pond, movement had started to come. First a ripple, a ripple, and a spasm of water. A fish-slap maybe, a carp lipping up a pond skater balancing on the frailty of the water's surface tension. But no. It wasn't any carp. There's wet hair now. There's a forehead now. There's a pair of eyes now.

Old Man Nacullian is rising out of the waters.

His face sallow with cold and his nose flattened and bent by breakage. Around his chin, barbs of silverblack stubble glisten and fleck. Wild sideburns are webbed with water and hands are prickled with browning freckles against the backdrop of his yellowed glabrous skin. At the slabbed edge of the pond, Old Man Nacullian rises to stand.

He is facing down. Pond lymph and pond weed all about him, all of him dipped, dripped languid as he comes to come forward. He walks haltingly, as if concentrating, intensely concentrating. The sleeves of this cotton shirt rolled up to the elbow, his trousered shanks silvered and waxed by deep water.

I should be waking soon, thought Cliff.

Old Man Nacullian halted forward and between the pond and the fence, stopped. The drips from him drank into the garden ground. Then, he raised his head to Cliff and spoke, with a voice oiled and popping with other places.

'The water is cold,' said the Old Man. 'And the woman belongs to me.'

This statement was terrifying enough for Cliff, and right after Old Man Nacullian said this, he was aware he should have woken by now, that normally he would have awoken by now. This speaking was the jolt and the signal to wake. But he did not wake, and his terror dripped into him.

'The water is cold,' said the Old Man. 'And the woman belongs to me.'

Cliff looked to the sky, which was still. He looked to the buddleia's leaves and the privet leaves and the beech leaves, which were still. The birdseed was still. He looked to the Nacullian's back door, which was closed. He looked into the misted glass panel of the door, to where no-one moved.

'The water is cold,' said the Old Man. 'And the woman belongs to me.'

Cliff thought he might trigger wakefulness by sliding back into his own garden, and so he pushed himself away and stepped down from the log.

'The water is cold,' said the Old Man. 'And the woman belongs to me.'

Perhaps he had forgotten to step down, had only thought about stepping down, had dreamt of stepping down. So, Cliff stepped down.

'The water is cold. And the woman belongs to me.'

And Cliff stepped down from the fence again.

'The water is cold. And the woman belongs to me.'

He tried to step down from the fence.

'The water is cold. And the woman belongs to me.'

Old Man Nacullian's eyes were like a jug of whey, but Cliff knew they beheld him squarely.

'The water is cold,' said the Old Man. 'And the woman belongs to me.'

This continued, Cliff stepping down from the fence and then finding himself back at the fence, with the Old Man saying again his devoted phrase.

A few centuries into this, Cliff had given up stepping down from the fence. All he could do was to stand there upon the threshold, listening to the man work his phrase in the same tone of gravel and undertow. Cliff began to worry that he would never wake up, and he would remain here with his old neighbour, being drenched in words until the faultless end of time.

Thankfully, Cliff always set an alarm. It had been about a millennium and three quarters into the dream when from the sky, the silent sky, his 7:30 alarm came down in the form of the throbbing plangence of the Bee Gees' 'How Deep is your Love?'. Barry Gibb sang unto Cliff.

♪ *I believe in you* ♫
♫ *You know the door to my very soul* ♪
♪ *You're the light in my deepest, darkest hour* ♫
♫ *You're my saviour when I fall...* ♪

Old Man Nacullian closed his milky eyes and winced a slow, cracking wince. Cliff looked to the buddleia's leaves, the privet leaves, the beech leaves, which spasmed in a sudden breeze. The old man buckled as if in terrible pain. At the bird table, a single sparrow flew in to feed. A terrible moan began from him. Cliff looked through the misted glass panel of the Nacullian's back door and saw a grey ripple of movement. He looked to the door itself, which was opening slowly.

It was Patrice, he knew.

'The water. Is...cold,' whispered Old Man Nacullian, as he dripped in globules out of Cliff's unconsciousness.

He was awake. 'Thank God for radio Solent', said Cliff, and patted the speaker of his alarm clock. His Mary was sitting up on the side of her single bed, her mask still over her, the wheezing and whirring of her machine fighting with the Bee Gees. She looked like she could do with her breakfast.

163

CHAPTER EIGHTEEN

An Interlude about Roads

It happens like this. Someone draws on a map. They draw a line, two lines, then a curve and a crescent. A little later on, a line, two lines, then a curve and a crescent are scratched into reality by people with pneumatic drills and diggers and all of the coarse and fine aggregates known to humankind. They make roads. Suddenly there are things like Mousehole Lane and White's Road and Pine Drive and Drowning Avenue. There are ring roads and residential roads and B roads and brick roads. This kind of thing is so common that we don't marvel at the movement from plan to reality. But give it a moment, because roads are all too easy to pass by.

Now while this is my city, I'm not one of those people who memorise road names. That kind of thing is only for taxi drivers and pedants and you know by now that I'm not a taxi driver or a pedant. Though it might not seem like it, not everything is available to me, and I don't know the names of all the roads just like I don't know how many times Matt Le Tissier played for Saints, or what really happened back in the Fifties when Niall Nacullian died.

Like in many places, the city's roads defy straightness. In this city a straight line is usually a dying thing, approaching a circle. Maybe in places that are so old or so small or so lazy, the land is not made anew when roads are built, but instead roads are fitted to the land, fitted around the land. Putting aside Shirley High Street, I like to think that the curves of our roads are the curves of our lands and that the rising and falling of our roads is the rising and falling of the earth beneath us.

Some people though don't draw curves and undulations on maps. Instead, they slap a gridiron down, a giant rebar of abstraction, and the digging and the drilling begins from there. But not in my city. Despite not having the grand dilapidation of Athens or the ornate intestines of Venice, this city is the cousin of those places where the roads are arteries and deltas, not gridirons and pointing fingers.

When it comes to the city's roads, there are some things you should know. When I sleep at night, I see the city's roads in me. They are the spaghetti of my soul. They are the arteries and the deltas. I can follow each thread, and often do. I travel through Bitterne and to Thornhill and into Harefield and out to Hamble. Sometimes I move my consciousness over the Itchen and into town, through the lull of Bevois Valley and then maybe a dandle through the quiet mediocrity of Portswood. I don't know the names of all these roads, but I see the life in them and I see the life that lines them.

I wonder and I wander. And as I do, time becomes as slippery as a pickled egg. Sometimes I'm seeing the solid wall of the present, but it's mortared by the past and I can't help but see it. Sometimes, all times seem laid on top of one another like sediment, and I have to stop and peer in to see the clay of this time or the limestone of that time. Seeing into time is a muddy thing.

Those trees produce fruit every year, though nobody picks them. That's the corner shop they robbed, countless times. Over there behind Warburton Towers are the woods with the old bomb shelters. That's the old carpet shop that only opened three weeks a year to sell fireworks. Down this road, a boy from Dumbledown Primary got run over by his teacher. And on this road, mothers stood out on their porches arguing about their kids. This is the posh street that always orders orange juice from the milkwoman. And this is the place the council flats were firebombed. On this road the prostitutes roamed up and down, though no one said anything about it. There was an ice-rink here. In that field, houses came. That pub over there was called the Swallows and was shut down for being a drug den. And over here the pub was demolished to build flats. Over this road, there used to be a footbridge connecting Thornhill and Sholing. And over there, Cobden bridge is closed for repairs. It was here on East Street the bomb went off. Over there, that shopping centre is shutting down. Up the road, the new shopping centre has just opened. That chippy does a good battered haddock. That café in St Mary's did a passable mixed grill. It's down that lane they said the murder took place. It's over there they say Slatty Kostek's sister was raped. To the left, he grew French beans on his allotment. To the right, she's digging up Maris Piper potatoes. The school up ahead once taught a paedophile who's in Winchester nick now. And behind the school, that chemist employed a lottery winner, before she quit.

So this is what my wonderings and wanderings can be like. My travels around the city's roads though are not random. I'll take one road and avoid the other. I'll look one way and not the other. And as everyone knows, a good narrator is nothing if not selective, and I'm here for the Nacullians, after all.

So when I wonder as I wander, the Nacullians are almost always there, among the sediments and layers of other people and other times. Over there's the General, where Greg was born. Just round the corner, a couple of years before, Nandad is on his third pint in the Brick and Mortar. Betty is buried over there in St Mochta's Churchyard and Shannon will live in that flat by Thornhill Park Road, one day. Patrice used to use that shortcut there on her way to the dentist with the kids. That's the memorial Cherry tree Bernard pissed on one time and was reported by Mary Clemens. Thunder ate a dead pigeon from that gutter by those shops. Greg was beaten up behind that substation by his mates and his tuck money was stolen. On that corner under a flickering lamppost, Shannon stuck her tongue deep into James Radley's left ear. That place just over there was the Royal Pier, where Patrice and Nandad went to dance on Fridays. Betty took Faiz's virginity somewhere over there in The Common. Up that alley, Thunder rubbed herself in another dog's shite. Nandad helped build that hall, which is gone now. Bernard helped to build those flats, which got refurbished last year. Shannon was a dinner lady there at Dumbledown. Patrice used to buy her fags from that shop and at that pharmacy, she bought her nicotine gum. And of course there's Kate-or-Rose just off Harbour Parade, looking at an information board about the old city walls. She's just been wandering down by the water, wondering about the RMS Titanic and the lore surrounding it and now, she's a little bored. She's reading about how these old walls defended against invading continentals, but it's just not Titanicy enough for her.

It's roads that make all this possible, but it only works for roads that defy straightness. In a gridironed city it's impossible to wander and wonder like this, because time goes too fast when it's in a straight line. Straight roads are leakers of time because there's an emptiness from one point to the next and then, unless you try very hard, the moment is gone.

My city's roads are the oxbows of time and the spaghetti of my soul. On the short road, the curving road, the residential road, time slows so it can be perceived. They are the artery and the delta. They are the sediment and the coarse and fine aggregates of the universe. Or if not the universe, then just the city. And in my city, I see time.

CHAPTER NINETEEN

The Fall
(2000)

It was her home and home was all that she had ever called it. After the death of her mother, Shannon Nacullian was still part of the family certainly, but she no longer knew which part she was. She could no longer see her role clearly, but we all know that families are impossible to see clearly, whatever we think we know about them.

'Baby-step the thing, Greg. No, don't drag it, baby-step it!' said Bernard.

'What d'you mean baby-step it?'

'God, you're useless, mush. Things'll be easier without you around.'

Half-scraping, half-waddling, Bernard and Greg edged a thin wooden wardrobe down the gravel driveway. Shannon watched them by a whiteish Luton van, its slide-door open.

'How many trips you think this'll take?' Shannon asked Bernard.

'All depends on what you want, Shan. If you just take what you need, then we'll be done round lunchtime. You said your place was part-furnished anyway. But if you want to drag out lots of

Mum and Dad's old crap, then we probably won't be done today, and I got work tomorrow over by the General.'

As a moving-in present to his sister and nephew, Bernard had borrowed a van from work without asking. When, on New Year's Eve Shannon had first suggested moving out, Bernard had made his offer of help with half-cut enthusiasm and millennial good will. On the TV, lights and fireworks and satellite feeds were embracing the cities of the world: In Auckland and Sydney, Tokyo and Hong Kong. In Seoul, Bombay and Moscow and Cario. In Johannesburg and Paris and London and Rio. And in Lima, in New York. San Francisco, Honolulu. When a man sees the world unfold like that, he can at least do someone a favour.

But later on, when she had decided the move was definite and had called in that favour, he cursed his half-arseholed offer. From what he could tell, the twenty-first century didn't deserve half of the enthusiasm the late twentieth century had poured into it. As far as Bernard could see, the days were the same, the streets were the same, the people were the same. The only thing people weren't doing now was getting all excited about the millennium. Yeah that was it, it was all the same as before, except for some reason no one was delivering the milk anymore.

In all honesty, leaving home for Shannon was anything but inevitable, and unless things are inevitable, you need an excuse or two. Shannon used many excuses about the reasons she needed to move, and while every excuse was a rickety thing, they were all a satellite of the truth.

'I can feel Mum and Dad in the house, and it gives me the shits,' was one.

'Greg's fourteen now and is growing up,' was another.

'I'm into my thirties now and want to grow up,' was used too.

Then there was, 'You'll be bringing women back, and I don't want to hear that.'

And also, 'What if I want to bring a man back? You don't want to hear that.'

Once she even said, 'Well it's inevitable, Bern, isn't it?'

Maybe if you added all of these excuses up, linked all the satellite feeds together, they'd be enough to show you the truth, but not quite completely.

But as well as borrowing a van from work, Bernard had also borrowed a former workmate of his, Christian Lovejoy, with the promise of minimal payment for a day of lifting boxes and baby-stepping cabinets up and down driveways.

'Christian's always broke cause they only give him the odd day here and there,' explained Bernard, as he slid the wardrobe into the van. 'Said I'd give him twenty quid in-hand and some chippy chips for lunch. So, I'll need that from you, Shan, plus the quid for the chips.'

Shannon pulled out her wallet from the inside of her puffy purple coat. She handed him four notes and began to fish for a coin in a one of the pouches. 'Isn't Christian the one who had you up in court for GBH?'

Bernard finished placing the wardrobe and straightened himself up. 'Yeah but that was ages ago, Shan. Water under the bridge.' He leaned in conspiratorially towards his sister, 'And he fucking started it, he did, putting that dogshit in my hat.'

Shannon smirked, 'Yeah, I do remember that now.'

'Lucky he didn't get crucified, treating me like that.'

She handed Bernard a pound coin. 'Spent a few weeks in hospital though, didn't he?'

'Yeah,' snorted Greg, and he pocketed the quid, before

reaffirming, 'but that's water under the bridge.'

As they stood by the van, Christian Lovejoy passed, and they both turned to watch him. Quiet and implacable, like time itself, he moved from house to van to house to van, seemingly with the minimum of sound or effort. The van was half full already.

'God. Looks like you got the right man for the job there, Bern,' said Shannon.

'Well,' said Bernard, quietly, 'he is one and he works like one.'

But Shannon had already left her brother's sphere, and was asking Christian whether he wanted tea or coffee, and how many sugars, and how much milk? Bernard watched them as they talked, halfway up the driveway. Then he watched as his sister headed back into the house with Christian.

'Someone needs to go get the chips for lunch!' shouted Bernard.

On the threshold, facing in, Shannon hesitated. 'Well, I'm not going.'

'Why the hell not?'

Her face remained turned away. 'I'm just putting the kettle on for Christian.'

'Tea can wait. Chris can do without tea. James is only open for another half hour.'

She turned to him, 'Look, I'll pay for the chips, but it's a bloody liberty I should have to pick 'em up too.'

'Well, then send Greg for the chips. He's half useless as it is, but he can do that at least.'

Another hesitation. Then, 'I think he's in the toilet. You know how long he takes in there.'

Shannon was right. Greg was in the toilet, sat down and leant forward and breathing heavily. He had been in there for some time now, partly because he didn't want to help with the move, but mainly because he was finding it very difficult to shit. He couldn't shake the image of his aunt Betty floating above him in the heavenly ether, along with his Nan and Nandad and God knows what other generations of Nacullians, all watching him take a shit, or failing to. Greg closed his eyes firmly and tried to imagine the bowel-loosening sound of foghorns. Yaffle ferry foghorns, RMS Titanic foghorns. Foghorns, foghorns, foghorns.

Still on the threshold, Shannon turned to her brother and simply said, 'You'll have to go, Bernard.'

Bernard threw his arms into the air, the way dickheads do when they think things are unfair, 'What's the fucking matter Shan? It's just chips!'

Shannon turned around, stepped through the doorway and back into the home.

Bernard went for the chips. Shannon had convinced him that he needed to pick up baccy at the corner shop anyway, and Greg was too young. Bernard though, had other suspicions. He hated having to walk up the hilly playing field towards the shop parade and he hated having to wait in line with Shannon's fiver to order four large chips and a saveloy.

'Four large chips and a saveloy,' said Bernard.

The man at the till turned very slightly to his right. 'Four large chips and a saveloy,' he said.

'James,' nodded Bernard.

'Bern,' nodded James.

Bernard paid and then stepped back to let the next order

through. The aroma of salt and fat and the flat tang of vinegar began to make him salivate, and he swallowed. He gave another nod to James, who did not nod back.

While Bernard had been initially enthusiastic about the idea of having the house to himself, on closer inspection, the proposal seemed less attractive. Sure, gone was the worry that he'd have to listen to his nephew having that wispy, panty poof-sex in his bedroom with gangs of other poofs. And gone too was the worry he'd have to listen to his sister fucking some random bloke she'd dragged back half comatose from The Garden Wall. But with his promise being called in, Bernard was realising just how much of a pain in the arse this moving business was. And maybe more than this, the closer moving-day had come, the less sure he was that he wanted the house to himself.

'You can take that bird feeder if you want. God knows I'm not going to feed the birds,' he had offered.

'The flat doesn't have a garden,' was Shannon's response.

Then a little later when Shannon had signed the contract with the council, she had said,

'Betty, then Dad and then Mum. Do you think about them, Bern?'

Bernard had hesitated. 'Spose,' he said.

'I do want to see you, Bernard.'

'Well Shan, you're always welcome back here if you want to, like, use the kitchen or anything.'

'My flat's got a kitchen, Bern,' his sister replied.

'Yeah, I know, but I just thought...'

'You're just wanting me to come over and cook you a fucking Sunday roast, is it?'

'Not just me. You could bring Greg too. If you wanted.'

Shannon had scoffed. 'You'll bloody struggle here without me, Bern.'

'What about you? Shitty little council flat, no job and fuck-all money.'

'Mum left me and Greg a little bit. And I've still got a few hours a week in Dumbledown.'

'Dumbledown? Christ. Mrs fucking Chips the dinner lady twice a week? You're going places.'

'I am going places,' said Shannon as she had walked away.

'Four large chips and a saveloy,' called James as he swung a bulging plastic bag onto the chip shop counter.

Because Shannon took less than she needed, they had only had to do one run and were parked up outside the flat a little after lunch. The Chippy Chips had been eaten before they left and the remains were now on the new second-hand kitchen table, blanketed in darkening chip shop paper. Somewhere in that bag, the fag end of a saveloy slumbered.

In the flat, Bernard and Christian were working fluidly, moving in and out of doorways and up and down corridors with the precision and speed of the committed. The job was now on and the pace was set, and the two men were quietly trying to outdo one another in the man-stakes. Shannon had been relegated to standing in the hallway and was saying where everything had to go. Kitchen, bathroom, bedroom, airing cupboard, Greg's room. Though smaller in build than Bernard, Christian moved with an economy and, a grace (was that it?), yes grace, that Shannon watched closely.

'He's married, Shan,' said Bernard, as he passed her with a box of towels. Though Christian wasn't married.

'Airing cupboard,' ordered Shannon.

'Got two little nippers too,' whispered Bernard, as he passed her with a clothes horse under one arm and a couple of fold-out chairs under the other. Christian had no children.

'Kitchen,' ordered Shannon.

If Shannon had been relegated, then Greg had been put into administration. He had been left in the little kitchen to sort the different pieces of cutlery into squeaky drawers. He was already done with this though and was just sat on one of the fold-out chairs, playing snake on his phone. He was doing quite well and was approaching his high score.

'Bathroom,' Shannon ordered Bernard.

'Bedroom,' Shannon said to Christian.

'Greg's room,' Shannon ordered Bernard.

'Bedroom,' Shannon said to Christian.

It was just before five when they stopped. In the man-stakes, Chris was convinced he had won and Bernard was certain he had won. I'm not sure who won, because I wasn't paying attention, but it was probably a draw.

Chris, Greg and Shannon were sat around the new second-hand table, fingering the leftovers of lunch and drinking tea.

'Look Mum,' said Greg. 'There's a bit of saveloy left. Can I have it?'

Shannon gave Greg a little nod and he whipped up the ruddy end of the sausage straight into his mouth.

Chris looked at the teenager munching happily on the cold butt. He watched the kid for so long, that he found both of them staring at him, mildly smiling.

'He looks like you,' said Chris, 'Got his mother's eyes. Nacullian eyes.'

'Well,' said Shannon, 'he is one. And he eats like one.'

Out in the hallway, Bernard had been pacing up and down as he nodded and hummed into his phone. Whenever he passed the doorway, he shot a glance into the kitchen, before going back to his nodding and humming. Then, as he passed the doorway again, he covered his phone with his hand and nodded to his sometime workmate.

'Chris mush,' said Bernard, 'There's a big job out in Botley if you're interested. Some millionaire's place. Got a bowling alley and swimming pool, they say. Looking for some labouring and landscaping.'

'You fucking with me? When was the last time you give me a tip?'

Bernard gripped his phone tighter. 'Well, I gave you this job, didn't I?'

Christian laughed and took a sip of tea, 'Bern, I know you ask Paul and Samson and all the rest. They got work already. Your very own Christian Lovejoy the only one left. The only one who works for twenty quid and chips.'

Bernard eyed Chris, as if about to argue. He would tell him to go fuck himself. He would drag him into the shell of some new shopping centre in town with a couple of his mates and put manners on him. Fucking bulging and splintered red manners, from him and his mates. He felt the urge to make a rollup, and maybe pick his nose. He looked at his sister and his nephew, sat there at the table with Chris. Somehow the image of them with their mugs of steaming tea and their lukewarm, vinegar-limp chips, gave him the desperate bowel-drenched belief that something was not fair.

'There's only one catch though, Chris. This Botley job, it's early work. Seven o'clock start and you live down by Northam, don't you? Be an early start for you then. But it's good work. Two weeks work, if you want it. They say he even lets you on the bowling alley.'

Chris understood, and looked down. Shannon understood, and looked up. Greg didn't understand, and blinked.

Bernard understood that Chris understood. He didn't know if Shannon understood. He understood Greg didn't understand. Leant against the doorframe, he began on a rollup.

'Ok,' said Christian, rising. 'Ok then. Call them and say I be there.' He looked at Shannon and then at Bernard. 'Your very own Christian Lovejoy better be going home.'

Christian Lovejoy left. It was quiet as Bernard finished making his fag.

'Well,' he said, 'gotta be off, sis. Early start for me over in Shirley.'

'Bern,' said Shannon.

'What?' said Bernard.

'You're a fucking cunt of a man, you know that?' she said. And this time, tears stung her eyes.

CHAPTER TWENTY

The Battle of Bitterne
(1986)

Several kinds of brick, was the answer.

Several kinds of brick was the answer to the question, 'What kinds of brick were used at the battle of Bitterne?' It's not that anyone has actually asked this question at any point, and it's not that anyone really remembers a hot day in the dead centre of 1986 when the battle took place between youths of the city's various council estates.

I remember it though, which is just as well, because I'm going to tell you about it. I'll try to be as accurate as possible, because to my knowledge there has not yet been any such account of the battle of Bitterne. It may be that some historian wishes to use this account as the basis for an original and fascinating study of the sociology of violence and local identity in the late twentieth century, and if she is so interested, I'd ask that she credit me.

So, let's begin with some basic facts before we get down to the shint and chiver of the battle. The ages of the combatants ranged from about 6 years old to around 15. After that age, there was an unwritten rule that you were too mature to be joining in with organised violence and you therefore had to stick to opportunistic and unplanned violence only. Oh, you could of course go looking for it, and the Thornhill 16-plus lot would go prowling about Sholing for just that reason. Likewise, the Bitterne over 16s would hang about the Harefield shops, scouting out opportunities to feel insulted.

Now this really was key. If you were over the age of 15, feeling insulted was your ticket to violence, because only little kids started hitting people without any provocation whatsoever. Here are some examples of the insults that would constitute a legitimate and instantaneously violent response:

1. Twat.
2. Your mum.
3. What you lookin' at?
4. Hello, I'm canvassing for the Conservative Party of Great Britain and Northern Ireland.
5. Oi mush, where you going?
6. (too much eye contact)
7. (too little eye contact)
8. (someone looking like a poof)
9. (someone looking like a bender)
10. (someone running away for no apparent reason)

So, everything on the list above was considered insulting, and would upset the 16-pluses of the city very much. If you followed this list or something like it, you'd be conducting yourself like an adult, because adults only hit cunts who deserved it and only when circumstances allowed for it. Below adult age no-one needed to be insulted in order to launch attacks on each other, as this fell into the broad and blood-filled category of play. The little kids of the city just ran around slapping each other about without any reason at all, and often at highly organised events, such as the Battle of Bitterne.

The time and place of the battle had been decided two weeks earlier, after a brief bit of barney and bone-picking on Bitterne High Street. Four ganglets from the local estates were throwing Happy Shopper cola and limeade about and giving each other a bit of kick and scram, when they all realised they needed to make some big plans, as the summer holidays were nearly there. They called out for a fifteen-minute truce to their skirmish and the four gang leaders met on the benches outside the greasy windows of the Baker's Oven café. While accounts differ, the leaders were most likely Becky Harrison (Thornhill), Jamie Watson (Bitterne), Bernard Nacullian (Harefield) and Aaron Kostek (Sholing). On those hallowed benches, the four leaders decided and agreed that they needed to finish this once-and-for-all, that each estate finally had to settle who was best once-and-for-all, that old grudges and old scores had to be put to rest once-and-for-all.

In two weeks then. By the church then. Once-and-for-all then.

Though this wasn't really once-and-for-all at all. Note later conflicts such as The Battle of Burgoyne Road (1987), Clash at The Common (1989), The Mansbridge Maimings (1992), The Thornhill Park Thrashing (1993) and The Hanny Rise Hangings (1994), to name but a few.

But that's what happened, anyway. In two weeks then. By the church then. Once-and-for-all then.

'Cry havoc and let slip the dogs of war!' cried Jamie Watson, who had stood up from the bench and raised both his fists into the air. The other leaders were quiet for a moment, as if impressed.

Then, Becky Harrison smacked a bottle into Jamie's face for being a wanker.

After this the gangs parted ways to prepare for the letting-slip of the dogs of war and to see out the school year. During those two weeks leading up to the battle, that generation of 6 to 15-year-olds learned a lot about teamwork, logistics, loyalty, patience, prudence, planning, diplomacy, foreshadowing, rhetoric, canvassing, sharing, metaphor, basic carpentry, bravado and bravery. While there was to be blood and bruises and hospital beds and fractures and food through straws and flids on crutches and spastics in wheelchairs, there was also a quiet undertow of significant educational gains. Though of course the kids didn't see the Battle of Bitterne in terms of educational gains. If they thought about the future at all, it was probably seen as practice for one day joining the ranks of the Mandela Boys, so they could go Paki-Bashing.

The Mandela Boys were a much feared and much admired bunch of racist thugs from over Freemantle way that even the black and Asian kids aspired to join. Tales of battles and clashes and maimings and thrashings hung about their reputation like the smell of petrol hangs about a moped in the woods before it's set on fire. The mystique of the gang was enhanced by the fact that no one really knew the names of individual Mandela Boys and no one knew how you became a Mandela Boy either. Likewise, no one knew how long the Mandela Boys had been going and no one ever really considered the idea that one day the Mandela Boys would become Mandela Men. All you needed to know was that the Mandela Boys were the Mandela Boys and they liked to go Paki-Bashing.

Now, if you had actually been lucky enough to come by the

Mandela Boys as you were roaming through Freemantle and you pointed out to them the irony of the fact that this racist bunch of thugs were called the Mandela Boys, they would doubtless tell you to fuck off before bashing you, Paki or not.

And if you pointed out to the Mandela-Boy-aspiring black and Asian kids that going 'Paki-Bashing' might involve beating up members of their own family or having to punch themselves repeatedly in the face whilst screaming racist slurs at themselves, then well, they would probably just tell you to fuck off before trying to bash you, whoever you were.

But back to the battle.

Several kinds of brick was the answer, the answer to the question no one was asking. To be more specific on the brick front though, the commoner sort of kid that took a brick as their weapon of choice went with your standard modular brick, because they didn't know any better and bricks were just bricks to them.

But the children of bricklaying families however did know better and were advised on less obvious but more effective kinds of brick. Bernard Nacullian, for example, had been well advised by this father to go with jumbo utility. More formidable-looking than the standard modular, surprisingly light and certainly hard enough to smash a skull or invert someone's nose into their face. While it wasn't the pretty kind of brick Nandad liked working with, the jumbo utility was a solid option for the inside of a cavity wall and Nandad respected it.

Becky Harrison's dad on the other hand said she should go with an 8" jumbo, as its size-to-weight ratio was just as good as the jumbo utility's, plus its breadth allowed it to double up as a shield. It was the brick of choice in the grimmer industrial projects about the city and Becky Harrison's dad got a special discount from the plant down in Swanage.

However, bricks, while popular, were not the only weapons at the Battle of Bitterne. A myriad of items were in use that day, including but not limited to, cricket bats and nailbats, coshes and stones, penknives and breadknives and paddles and rulers, hammers and staplers, corkscrews, screwdrivers, and beer bottles, milk bottles, cheese graters, cheese wires.

To be clear on the matter then, there were four main combatant groups involved in the Battle of Bitterne. The boys from Bitterne itself, which included girls, the Sholing lads which included ladettes, Harefield mushes which included mushovas and the mateys from Thornhill, which included matesses. The families of these four groups were constituted by, but not limited to, the following:

Bitterne	Thornhill
The Kerinses	The Bakers
The Lovejoys	The Brennans
The Headers	The Alsaids
The Watsons	The Curtains

Harefield	Sholing
The Nacullians	The Harrisons
The Masons	The Kosteks
The Jordans	The Winters
The Radleys	The Dunkfords

These families only mapped roughly onto one of the four estates. For example, the Kerinses were mostly Bitterne-based, but Dani Kerins had moved to Harefield in 1979, so it was expected that her two kids would represent Harefield in battle. Likewise, the Radleys were from Harefield in the main, but it was rumoured that more than a couple of women from Thornhill and Sholing had sprogged on James Radley's behalf, and so there was a question as to loyalties.

So, imagine this philosophical conundrum on the field of battle where a Kerins from Bitterne meets a Kerins from Harefield. Would you smash a cousin up with your rounders bat? Would you hand-hammer staples into the forehead of your half-sister? Would you put a broken bottle into the face of a slavering Alsatian owned by your uncle? All of these are difficult moral questions and if you asked them to any of the affected kids, well, they'd probably tell you to fuck off, before trying to bash you.

The battle took place in and around the mildewed and monumented grounds of St Mochta's Catholic Church, a flint-flanked sanctuary buttressed between The Garden Wall pub on one side and a supermarket carpark on the other. The collective decision on location was not because a church had the requisite gravitas and solemnity for such a once-and-for-all occasion, but because the kids were most likely to fight undisturbed amongst the gravestones, which themselves provided cover against bricks and bottles. And as a side benefit, the parents who wanted to could enjoy the action from the pub, on what was forecast to be a scorcher.

So, the sun rose fresh and rosy fingered on the day of the Battle of Bitterne. Across the kitchens of Bitterne and Harefield and Thornhill and Sholing, 6 to 15-year-olds munched on non-branded wheat biscuits and flakes of corn, and they slurped at glasses of orange squash and semi-skimmed milk. Then they were out the door, walking, bussing, running, cycling and all converging on Bitterne High Street.

Now, it had been agreed previously that each estate would assemble in a different area of the churchyard. If memory serves, Bitterne began near The Garden Wall pub and the Sholing lot started by the supermarket carpark. Thornhill gathered in the east and Harefield mustered to the south. The battle was to commence at noon, or when the first brick was thrown, whichever was the earlier. It was understood by all that the following general rules applied:

1. Latecomers would be admitted.
2. Dogs could be maimed but not killed.
3. No switching sides.
4. No stealing from the bodies of the fallen.
5. Anyone outside the walls of the churchyard are classed as spectators.
6. Spectators could not be directly attacked, but could be targeted with missiles.
7. The leader of each estate can call for one timeout during the battle (3 minutes).
8. Anyone breaking the timeout rule receives one free hit.
9. Paramedics within the church grounds are legitimate targets.
10. Go home when you get bored.

Across the road from the churchyard, The Garden Wall afforded superb views of the action, and some dads had taken the day off sick to watch their sons, which included daughters, prove themselves amid the moss and gravestones. They clustered amiably around the tables at the side of the pub, well supplied with cold pints and fresh crisps and clean ashtrays.

'Cry havoc, and let slip the dogs of war!' screamed Jamie Watson from the Bitterne starting box. He charged into the centre by the church's northern buttresses, waving his standard modular brick above his mousey head. Jamie looked to the east and scanned the west and peered through the tombstones to the south and from everywhere, there came a murmuring, gathering sigh.

Then from the south, a balloon of piss exploded against the buttress, dousing him.

From the west, a milk bottle grazed his mousey scalp.

Then from the east, Becky Harrison came and decked the wanker with her 8" jumbo.

And the Battle of Bitterne had begun.

They walked on the graves of ancestors and strangers, the bones of jazz saxophonists and the ashes of mediocre bricklayers. Aside from the occasional wet-faced mourner knelt at the graveside of their relative or lover or friend, the children were unimpeded and while the rules were not explicit on the matter, mourners were considered legitimate targets. They ran through the dead floral tributes of regret and over the plastic memorial trinkets of woe. They toppled over the damp photographic representations of better days and they wiped their dog-shit shoes on the empty plots of the future, because they were children.

Alice Header (general attack, Bitterne) gave a good sharp kick to the balls of Sean Mason (general defence, Harefield), who only thirty seconds beforehand had grated a chunk of cheek off Abdul Alsaid (Thornhill all-rounder). Abdul had in turn just recently bottled Slatty Kostek (reserve, nominally of Sholing), who was only passing on his way to the shop to buy biscuits for his sweet old babcia.

Naturally at the Battle of Bitterne, Bitterne had the home advantage. Though on the other hand, the Harefield and Thornhill and Sholing lot knew that Bitterne had the home advantage, so they targeted the Bitterne lot all the more. The general effect was to break even.

And another interesting fact, the brown kids got 25% more violence than the white kids, and the girls got 25% less shint and chiver than the boys because, you know, they were girls. At the Battle of Bitterne then, racism and sexism conspired to balance out and if you were a brown girl, you basically broke even, which is unusual in life really.

But the Battle of Bitterne was happening, it was the bleeding edge of the present, it was the aching tooth of now. Imagine a bunch of BAMs and POWs and SMAAAKs with colourful spikey boxes around them and lots of exclamation marks like you get in comics. This was the Battle of Bitterne, only real. Amid the brickbats, pissbombs and shouting, insults and punches and scrapes, between the barks and bites and hammerings, the smashing, pushing and cleaving, came a voice.

'Oi Bernie!' shouted this voice, as it looked down at something, 'This your sister here? The mad one?'

Bernard Nacullian was three gravestones away, nursing a swollen eye and attempting to sharpen his jumbo utility unsuccessfully on a piece of flint. When the voice came he pretended not to hear and decided to even more actively focus on the sharpening of his brick.

Gabriella Dunkford was kicking and scramming a piebald mongrel out of the grounds. Dave Jordan was fending off someone's Ball Python with his cricket bat, but the voice of the boy continued, 'Says here on the stone she's a Na-Hooligan, Bernie, like you. So what did Bet...?' the voice continued.

But any further line of questioning was halted by a brick from three gravestones away that split both lips and took out three teeth. If you were paying attention, you'd have noted that it was a jumbo utility brick. There was a red torrent and a gargled claim of friendly fire from a blood-filled mouth that no one could understand.

A few days later, Bernard Nacullian would claim this was around the time when he got bored and went home. This stuff was for kids, he would say. And it was only kids went about slapping people about for no reason.

No one was quite sure when the battle of Bitterne ended, but the results, as near as anyone can tell, were as follows:

Thornhill claimed Thornhill had won.

Harefield said that Harefield had won.

Sholing swore Sholing had won.

Bitterne knew Bitterne had won.

Which basically means everyone broke even.

CHAPTER TWENTY-ONE

The Round
(1999)

4 a.m. in summer is the loneliest time on earth. I've heard there are people who wake themselves from a natural and perfectly amicable sleep and walk outside to hear the dawn chorus. They exalt in the blackbird's song, the sparrow's chirrup and the skylark's liquid trills in distant yellow fields.

These people are liars. They're liars because what these people are really after is loneliness. In summer at 4 a.m. there is no one in the city, and you can suddenly see how alone you are. When you're alone in the dark, you can always imagine an ally is nearby, just about to embrace you and offer comfort. But in the daylight, no such pretention exists. The dawn-chorus people are liars because they desire to be lonely, but they cover this over by pretending to like birdsong. With the possible exception of addled Channel Islanders tottering outside the city airport or clubbers who spent their taxi fare on another pill, no one is out at 4 a.m. unless they desire loneliness.

Except of course the milkman, or the milkwoman, which is the case here, because this is a story about a milkwoman and this is most definitely a story. If at any time this story seems to impinge on reality or mirror a fact you know to be the case, then you may take it that your narrator has failed you.

The name of the milkwoman was unimportant, and if the Nacullians didn't know her name then there's no reason you should know either. The milkwoman had been working her round for about four years, the kind of timescale where you know exactly and intimately what you need to do but not long enough that you're so sick of it that you leave or die trying.

This day when the milkwoman was about her business was a time in history when the mobile milk industry was in a desperate old state. This was principally because of out-of-town supermarkets. Out-of-town supermarkets, those castles of glass and white metal, had just about sucked the teat dry of the mobile milk industry, until the mobile milk industry was scraping by on the milk of human kindness, or the curds and whey of old-time sentimentality, or whatever. You see, in the late 1990s, people started to realise that in the place where they bought everything else apart from their milk, they could buy their milk.

When people realised they could buy their milk in the same place they bought everything else, it was like the start of a great famine for the mobile milk industry. For many decades, the mobile milk industry had been using mind control and insistent early-morning whistling to successfully keep this startlingly obvious fact from the public, but by the late 90s, the game was up.

Since the milkwoman had first begun her round, she had noticed a pattern. Her round had steadily expanded over the east of the city as the number of customers and orders had steadily decreased. Even the middle classes had stopped ordering orange juice. This simultaneous expansion and contraction had led to a lighter milk float and a heavier mileage. Starting at 3.a.m, crossing Northam bridge, the Itchen dark and bulbous beneath you, through Bitterne, coming up through the back of Sholing and into Thornhill, then Harefield and back to the depot.

All of this took time in a milk float that was capable of a maximum speed of 9mph. A long time. And the milkwoman had learned early on that you either go mad or you accept the pace you're given. She'd once caught a programme about medieval pilgrims on Channel 4 and was amazed at how they put up with all that walking and didn't just pack the lot in. Ah, but there were no milk floats in 1448 she thought, and the comparison made her feel better. Her Rangemaster milk float was a fine machine in many ways, but still, this was the end of the twentieth century and going around at 8mph through the summer loneliness felt, well, slow. Sometimes, she imagined being back in 1448 on her milk float. She would be crossing the Itchen on a rickety wooden bridge and the pilgrims would stare at her in wonder on their long and pointless walks to Salisbury, or Canterbury, or Winchester. She might have been slow, but by God she was faster than a 1448 pilgrim.

The milkwoman was coming into Harefield now, the last part of the round. Despite the general decline in sales there were a few families around the city who had remained stalwartly loyal to the mobile milk industry, and in the tiny DairyDart© messroom in Northam industrial estate, the dwindling milkies would whisper the names of their loyal families over large mugs of milk:

Winterbottom, they would whisper.

Dunkford, they would whisper.

Harrison, they would whisper.

For the milkwoman, her city was a series of direct lines

between her loyal families, lines that defied the bends and curves of the city's roadways and cut through brick and water and sky. Whilst her early morning shifts made sure she never actually saw these families, her fancies regarding who they were and what they were like were unreasonably derived from their houses and their orders. The Dickenses for example were an Itchen family with a detached four bed redbrick just off the main road. The shape of the numbers on their door gave her the odd idea that they were a square and stout family with curly black hair. They ordered two pints of skimmed and a pint of orange juice every day, and always washed out their empties.

The Lovejoys' house was different. A terraced one-up-one-down kind of place just over the bridge, it was the milkwoman's first stop. It had a tiny concrete scrape which separated the door from the Bitterne Road and plastic little white numbers had been drilled into the brick wall. It was one full fat pint three times a week for the Lovejoys, and this gave the milkwoman the image of a middle-aged man who ate cereal late at night. In fact, the milkwoman suspected that the Lovejoys were probably just a lone and solitary Lovejoy.

And then there were the Nacullians. They were now one of only two dozen or so orders in Harefield, and after the Nacullians, there were only four more to tick off before heading back to the depot, then home. Their house was a neat little council terrace with slim black numbers nailed to a white wooden plaque beside the front door. The milkwoman had the suspicion they were a shy and reliable family, well turned-out with children with finely combed hair. They went for two greentops five times a week.

Occasionally, the milkwoman would look up at the Nacullian's place to see a little light on in the top bedroom, and the curtains drawn back. This had only happened in the last year or so, four or five times maybe, and gazing up at the room's artexed ceiling she would notice ripples of movement play with the light which shrouded the room. This morning the curtains were drawn back, but there was no sign of the usual movement.

With a slowing whirr and chorus of clinks the Rangemaster came to a halt by the neat little house. The milkwoman stepped off and found the Nacullian's order in the usual place. Two greentops were in an otherwise empty crate. She ambled up the short gravel driveway and placed the bottles by the front door. There were two clean empties to take, and she took them silently and without thinking.

A quickening whirr and another chorus of clinks. The Bensons, two bluetops. The Kerinses, a pint of blue and two redtops. The Smiths, one greentop. The Phos, two blue. There. All done and all ticked.

Back in Northam at the DairyDart© depot, the milkwoman was unloading. She went round to the back of the float to unload the crate of empties. Against the clarity of empty glass, a piece of paper was visible, rolled up into the mouth of one bottle.

'Another cancellation,' she said to herself and she slid the tube of paper into the rough cotton pocket of her uniform. She wondered why they had to wear uniforms at all, as no one ever really saw them. But it was company policy, and maybe she wouldn't have felt the same delivering milk in jeans and a jumper. Maybe that would look like someone planting milk outside someone's house, rather than someone delivering the stuff. No, she thought, uniforms were safer all round.

With the crate in her hands she walked over toward a frail-looking staff portacabin where a little wall of crates was forming. When she placed the crate with the others, a tintinnabulation rippled through the stack before edging off into the quiet of the yard. Just beyond the depot, she could hear the occasional high hiss of traffic as it crossed Northam bridge. She headed through the portacabin door and into the messroom.

The messroom was almost empty, as it usually was. Gary, a colleague who covered the city centre and was always back first, was sitting in a worn leather chair at the far end of the room. He was bent over slightly and his ear was cemented to a transistor radio he held in one hand. He nodded to the milkwoman as she came in and went back to his ardent listening.

Tired now, the milkwoman waded over to the kitchen area and opened the staff fridge. Nearly out of milk again. She held the remains of a bluetop up to the florescent lights and shook it slightly. A sediment of curds shifted down, leaving a misty translucence of whey above. She would make do with black coffee.

With a background of fuzz from Gary's radio, she sat down at one of the plastic messroom tables. Her mug was a souvenir one of the milkies had brought from some holiday or other. It was white and read Bell Island Community Museum in bland black lettering. Outside in the yard, she could hear the asthmatic creak of another float arriving at the depot.

The milkwoman took a sip from her mug and winced at the too-hot coffee. She put the mug down and reached into her rough cotton pocket. She fished out the paper and unfolded it. The text was tight and careful and the milkwoman had to read slowly.

Dear Mrs Milkwoman,

I have decided I need to tell you something, because no one in my family listens to me anymore. Now, this isn't one of those funny letters, this is a woman writing to you now, so don't go fearing I'm going to go saying something disgusting to you. I've watched you on your milk float there going up and down the street for some time now. In the mornings I sometimes look out, and you never seem to look up. I like it this way, as you seem like a busy, happy woman delivering all that milk, and the early morning is a fine part of the day, is it not? Especially in the summer.

You know I think it's amazing that they let a woman deliver the milk, and I think you must be so proud to be a milkwoman when everyone else is just a plain old milkman. You deliver that orange juice too, don't you? I've often thought I'd like to order the orange juice, but it's expensive, isn't it? And it seems like such a well-to-do thing, doesn't it? Whatever the case is, it's too late to try it now.

Because you see I'll be dying tonight and you know the funny thing is, that by the time you read this, I'll be dead. That's the phrase, isn't it? That's what they say on the TV and suchlike? Sounds funny writing it down, but I'm not trying to be all dramatic or anything, I'm just trying to say something to someone who'll take a bit of notice. God knows I've tried to tell my family I'm going, but there's no getting through those thick skulls of theirs. It's all because of all these things and stuff they've got about them. There's so much of it that they're going blind. They can't see what it is that's important, but there's me moralising again, and I know my Shannon hates that.

So I'm dying tonight and if you want to know how I know, then you'll just have to believe me that it is what God intends. I'll not be doing anything but going to sleep and I know that I'll not be waking up. I keep thinking about you reading this Mrs Milkwoman and of you reading the words of a dead woman. I'm not trying to be morbid now, but it's a funny thing, isn't it, to be dead? And I suppose that's why I need to be writing you this note, whatever you think of it.

I'm so sorry to have jabbered on like this at you, but I needed to express myself before my time comes. And I can feel that it is coming. Anyway, I'm sure you're a very busy a woman with all your milk and your orange juice and whatnot. I can't tell you how much I respect a woman being a milkwoman. Good for you. I'm sure your children must be very proud of you.

With kind regards and warm wishes,
Patrice Bernadette Nacullian

P.S: And please cancel our order from now on. It turns out you can buy milk cheaper in the supermarket.

'Shit,' hissed the milkwoman, and flattened the paper out on the table.

Gary glanced over to her. 'What is it?' he whispered, his ear still stuck to the fuzzing speaker of the little radio.

The milkwoman took a sip of her coffee before she spoke. Still too hot. 'It's the Nacullians.'

'Oh,' said Gary. 'What about the Nacullians?'

'The old woman only went and cancelled on me,' she said, and blew across the black surface of the coffee. 'I tell you Gary, things only go from bad to worse around here.'

Gary was quiet of a moment and was nodding solemnly. 'I'm very sorry to hear that,' he said, and then went back to his radio.

CHAPTER TWENTY-TWO

An Interlude About Sky

You might think that there is little to say about a city's sky. A city's sky isn't really part of the city, you might opine. There's such a thing as airspace, you'll agree. There's British airspace, Turkish airspace, Russian airspace, yes. But there's no such thing as Cwmbran airspace, or Coventry airspace or Hull airspace. The city and the sky are two different places, you're sure.

Well, you're just an ignorant shite if you believe that. I don't mean to be rude, but it's a subject I'm passionate about. People spend their lives wandering about, looking up there, as if up there is somewhere else altogether. They do this to feel they are escaping the city, probably because they hate the city, but they're not escaping it at all. The sky is as much a part of the city as its roads, or its water or its parks or its history.

The situation is somewhat unfair to the poor old sky that sits above this city. Take the sewers, for example. They are beneath the city like some vast subterranean network that carries shite. They're important, sewers are, and they are part of the city, you'd agree. And we're willing to accept this area of the city as the city, even though it's hidden from us. But not so for sky, even though we can see it up there, in the sky.

But it's the sky that makes the night in the city, and the day in the city. The city's night is made in the sky, and the floppy romance of its parks are aided by the pinks and ambers of the city's gloaming. When the fug of fog descends and schleps down the city's streets, the sky is walking on the street and when the rain comes, as it often does here, the sky is sweating in the hot faces of the city dweller, though they do not know it.

It is true that you can, by human ingenuity, bring the sky closer, or at least seem to bring it closer. This is because of skyscrapers. Skyscrapers scrape the sky and pull it down, bring it closer to the denizen, to form a visible bridge between them and it. Once in the early 80s Nandad was offered a spot of work up in London building a skyscraper, a brickless erection of glass and metal meant to house a retail bank or a merchant bank or an investment bank. But the lack of bricks and the proximity to a number of the parkish parks of London put him off, and he turned the job down.

Unlike a London sky or a Brummie sky or a Tokyo sky, the sky in my city though is not very close. The sky is so low in Tokyo, because its buildings are so high. The sky of my city though seems high, because most of the buildings are in the low-to-medium category. You'll remember our Titanicy tourist Kate-or-Rose, who's been hanging about the city for a while now because she's so incredibly fond of the RMS Titanic and the lore surrounding it. Well, as she was first coming into the city on the train from airport parkway, she noted these low-and-medium sized buildings and thought they were hardly befitting the grandeur of the city where the Titanic set off on its ill-fated voyage blah blah blah. Later on though, as she was boarding a flight to Cork, the last stop of the Titanic blah blah blah, she did look up and noted that the sky here was very high.

The height of the sky in this city results in our citizens looking up at it more than a Londoner or a Brummie looks up, and makes the sky seem to be even less a part of the city, because it just seems to be up there, in the sky. Though the sky is of course as much a part of the city as its roads, or its water or its parks or its history.

Betty Nacullian was one for the sky, I remember. From about the age of 12 she'd wonder about looking upward without paying a blind bit of attention to what was happening round her. She'd look at the sky no matter what kind of sky it was. If it was a crystalline-blue spring firmament or the sloppy stew of a November sky, it made no difference. It's hard to say if she was bored or was looking for deliverance or just had a bad neck, but she was constantly smacking into things and nearly got run over a few times.

Now we sometimes say, by which I mean that you people sometimes say, that we all live under the same sky. This is meant to encourage the idea that people in the city are really just like those in Tokyo or London or Portsmouth. It's the kind of abstract and sentimental notion that only someone looking at a map could conceive of, because maps are shallow, flattering things. Have you seen the sky in Beijing? Have you smelled the sky in Dundalk? No, we don't live under the same sky, and those lovers of the one-sky idea could never see our sky for what it is, as part of the city.

So, don't look up at the sky and ever think you escape. Because you see, you aren't linked to the rest of humanity by the sky and no matter how high the sky, you'll never escape the city by looking up. That's the way of madness. If you really want to escape, get on a fucking train mush.

CHAPTER TWENTY-THREE

Flames
(2002)

Some kids from Dumbledown Primary were singing. Well, they weren't actually singing, it was more of a high monotone drone that all kids do because they can't really sing. You might know it yourself. It goes,

♪ *Remember remember the 5th of November* 🎵
🎵 *Gunpowder, treason and plot!* ♪
♪ *I see no reason why gunpowder treason* 🎵
🎵 *Should e-ver be for-got!* ♪

Parents looked on with pride or annoyance or those mild smiles parents use to hide indifference. Once they had finished singsaying this, they started it again, each time with more energy and less suggestion of melody.

♪ *Remember remember the 5th of November* 🎵
🎵 *Gunpowder, treason and plot!...* ♪

Parents looked on with annoyance or those mild smiles

parents use to hide indifference. The kids started again, again with more energy and less suggestion of melody.

♪ *...I see no reason why gunpowder treason* 🎵
🎵 *Should e-ver be for-got!* ♪

Parents looked on with annoyance and then pulled their swaddled children away with promises of sparklers and hotdogs.

The Thornhill bonfire happened every year in the big field out the back of the old community centre. People from the local estates would come down for the blaze and the accompanying fireworks display. The event was never advertised, there were no tickets and no-one knew or cared if it had been sanctioned and signed-off by the city council. However, the gaggle of lurching men in hi-vis vests and the semi-circle of burger vans flanking the field gave everything an air of legitimacy. People automatically turned up because this had been happening since anyone could remember, and it only happened at all because people automatically turned up.

The central slip of the field was reserved as the display ground and cordoned off with sagging red-and-white tape wrapped around the occasional wooden peg. Beyond the cordon was the land of the hi-vis men, who ran about lighting rockets and fountains and Catherine Wheels and long red lines of firecrackers seemingly at random. Occasionally, the hi-vis men would become even more hi-vis when a Catherine Wheel would spiral out of control or a lit rocket teeter and fall to the ground before take-off.

Towards the back of the field they would build the bonfire, though who 'they' were was something of a mystery, or at least it would have been a mystery if anyone had bothered to ask.

The construction was a skeleton of pallets stuffed, bolstered and braced with whatever could be found around the local area. The back of the odd chair or table leg could be seen sticking out of the inferno and it wasn't unusual to find old bathroom cabinets or unwanted bookshelves added to the blaze. Every year there would always be a family or two who drove down to donate their excess broken crap to be burnt for the sake of the community. It was generally understood that playing a kind of eye-spy with burning objects was all part of the traditional fun, and every year was different.

This year for example, a kid of about seventeen had spotted something. He was hopping up and down and pointing at the blaze.

'Fuck! That's my moped! Got stole last week. They're burning my fucking moped.'

A few in the crowd squinted at the gathering pyre and nodded that yes, there was a moped in there.

As they did every year, the Nacullians came up from Harefield to watch the display. It was a cold night and Shannon had dragged a grumbling Greg the half hour walk through the estates.

'Bet Uncle Bernard won't even bother to turn up,' complained Greg.

'Well he said that he would,' said Shannon as they made their way through the dark pillars of Thornhill woods.

'You know your Nandad used to bring us all up here every year when I was a kid,' said Shannon as they approached the back of the circling food vans. 'He said they used to have great big bonfires back in Ireland when he was young. We always had a laugh here. Even Betty liked it.'

'And what about Nan?'

'Oh, she never came with us. Said it was against Catholics or something.'

'Is it?'

Shannon shrugged. The smell of bonfire hit them, a cocktail of woodsmoke, plastic and petrol mixed with slippery redolence of hot meat and oil from the vans.

The pops and crackles of the crowd could be heard now.

'What you want to do first then Greg? Want a sparkler?'

'Mum, I'm sixteen? You think I want a sparkler?' Greg shoved his chin a little further into his coat.

'Well what do you want to do then?'

'Said before, didn't I? Just go home.'

'You just want to play on your bloody computer,' said Shannon, 'I know what you're like.'

'So what? It's fucking cold here and we don't know anyone.'

Shannon's eyes widened and she threw a slap across Greg's hood. 'Don't you fucking swear in front of me. And course we know people. We know everyone.'

And here Shannon scanned the shadowed mass of forms for an ember of recognition. There was a pause.

'Look!' she said and pointed over towards one of the burger vans. 'There he is. There's your Uncle Bernard. Told you.'

Bernard was on his own, concentrating on squirting mustard into a long hotdog. As Shannon and Greg approached, he nodded, opened his mouth wide and shot a third of the hotdog into his gob.

'Alright there, little brother,' said Shannon as she came up to him.

'Ve gymos ere ave onw gnot meran mussar, inch an en weaw mussar,' chewed Bernard.

'What the bloody hell you saying?'

Bernard rolled his eyes and continued his chewing impatiently. He finished with a great cartoon swallow.

'I said, the gypos here have only got American mustard, which ain't even real mustard. Proper English mustard is what this needs,' Bernard said as he waved two-thirds of hotdog at his sister.

Shannon folded her arms at Bernard. 'So, no hello for me then?'

Bernard shrugged and gave a little, 'Alright sis.'

'Hello Bern,' said Shannon and she leaned in to give him a peck. From behind her, Greg stepped forward.

'Uncle Bernard,' said Greg.

'Greg,' said Bernard.

Before a Nacullian silence could take hold, the display began. The first fireworks went screaming up into the sky. They silenced the repeated drone of the Dumbledown kids and soon after, somewhere up there, they burped and spluttered with green sky-tinsel.

'Oooooooooo....,' sighed the crowd.

After a few more volleys, the Catherine Wheel was next. The spectators crowded close into the sagging cordon, as one hi-vis man held a lighter at the end of his arm, toward the base of a dark wheel. For a few seconds nothing seemed to be happening, and then a spark took hold and the wheel shuddered into revolution. The hi-vis man bounded away into the darkness as the spluttering reds changed to circles of silver sparks.

'Why do they call it a Catherine Wheel?' asked Greg.

'How should I bloody know?' said Shannon.

Bernard snorted and shook his head. He shoved the last third of the hotdog into his mouth.

'Meran mussar, an en weaw mussar,' he said.

Greg's face was ensconced in his coat, his head directed down toward his feet and the muddy field under him. It stayed that way as a battery of gold spirals braided over the field and towards the derelict community centre.

'Oooooooooo....,' sighed the crowd.

'You know Cliff from next door?' said Bernard, as he gazed half-lidded at the exploding sky.

'Oh yeah, Cliff Clemens the bus driver,' Shannon nodded, 'One that fancied Mum.'

Bernard slackened his bottom lip, but did not turn round. 'Did he?'

'You never noticed? Was always on top of that fence when Mum was out the back.'

Bernard's response was flat. 'Dad would have taken his balls if he'd known.'

A white flock of swan's necks hissed into the black.

'How is old Cliff then?' asked Shannon.

'Dead.'

She turned to her brother. A ragged phalanx of rockets shot screaming fire upwards.

'Ahhhhhh...,' gasped the company.

Bernard sniffed at the cold, 'Saw the paramedics taking the body out,' he continued, 'Was covered over. Place is for sale now.'

'Shame,' said Shannon.

'Spose,' said Bernard.

A fat firecracker was tossed by a hi-vis man into the mass of spectators. People tittered and squealed and scattered as the firecracker bounced and fizzed among them, coming to explode with a deep percussive pop between the legs of Manu Alsaid. Manu let out a shrill cry of pain and fear and buckled over, grabbing her blasted calves. She was loving it.

'And what about Mary?' asked Shannon.

'Who?'

'Mary. His wife.'

'Oh, the shut-in. Don't know. Maybe it was her they took out then. But Cliff's not there now, is all I know.'

Helixes of dappling blue bristled cloudward. Even Greg looked up.

'Beautiful, aren't they?' said Shannon.

Bernard shrugged. 'Women think everything's beautiful. What worries me is we've got all these explosives about and now the Muslims are on the warpath.'

'Oh, fuckssake Bernard, don't start on that.'

'They're after our buildings Shan, that's what they're doing. They'll take us down one building at a time.'

Kids gazed in awe at sparklers that were inches from their face.

'Well, I wouldn't care if they blew up the old community centre there. It's been sat there doing sod all for ages now.'

Bernard continued to look sleepily upward. 'One building at a time,' he murmured.

The bulk of another body squeezed in on Shannon's right. At first, Shannon didn't think anything of it, but she noticed that the form kept turning away from the display, towards her direction. Then she saw who it was.

'You want another hot dog?' Shannon blurted to Bernard.

'What?'

'Fancy another hot dog?'

'What, you buying then, are you?'

'Yeah,' said Shannon as she fumbled a tenner out from her leather purse. 'And take Greg with you and buy him one too.'

Behind them, Greg looked silently at the back of the form next to his mother.

'You want mustard on yours, Shan?' asked Bernard.

'Look, I don't care. Just take him and go buy 'em!'

'No need to be a bitch,' snorted Bernard, but then he saw who was next to Shannon, and gave a nod of recognition.

'C'mon then, Greg,' he said as he lightly pushed the shoulder of his nephew, 'Let's see if we can get some English mustard round here. Not that you'd be able to handle it.'

And with that he led the boy away.

'Shannon Nacullian,' said the form.

'What is it, James?'

'Been a long while now. Just think we should be civil is all. Like, what is it, twenty years?'

'Seventeen.'

'S'what I mean, right? Water under the bridge over troubled water. Or whatever.'

Shannon kept her view on the fireworks ripping up and scalding the sky.

'You're looking good, Shannon,' said James.

'Don't try that. I'm just another gullible munter to you.'

He turned away from the display and towards her.

'Woh, that's a bit harsh, int it? And I never called you a munter.'

'To my face, you didn't.'

James stalled slightly. Shannon turned her head to the left, to check if she could still see Bernard and Greg.

'Anyway, whatever you say, I think you're looking good.' He shot a look over Shannon's shoulder. 'So, what're you up to now?'

Shannon sighed. And maybe because she was bored or awkward or polite, she told him. Shannon outlined what she had been up to for the past seventeen years or so. And as she talked, James Radley nodded and smiled and waited and in no way listened to her.

'So yeah,' said Shannon, who had now turned her body slightly toward him, 'That's about it really. What about you?'

'Well, it's like this. My Emily walks out on me a couple of years ago and takes my youngest with her. Won't speak to me no more. Won't even answer my calls or my texts. Nothing. Cold turkey she is. The bitch turned my youngest on me too. They're both changing their names now, they are. Going back to Header. My ex making my youngest lose her rightful name,' and here he shook his head with genuine solemnity.

As he talked, Shannon nodded and waited and was in no way surprised.

'So,' she said when he had finished, 'That why you talkin' to me now then, is it?'

'God Shan,' and here James threw up is hands into the night, 'You must think I'm an absolute total cunt of a man, don't you?'

Shannon shrugged, but she was smiling now. He had got her smiling.

'Well, I can't say I blame you,' he said with a grin.

'No?' This time she looked at him.

'So, you know, just want to say I'm sorry for the past and all that.'

'Yeah?'

'Yeah.'

And then suddenly, James stepped back from Shannon and stuck his hand out, open palmed, in front of him. Without moving her head, Shannon flicked her eyes down at the offering and back up to James, who was still smiling.

Shannon let out an exasperated sigh, but she slid her hand forward. James grasped it and they shook, up and down, in several slow exaggerated undulations.

'And I just want to say,' he announced as Shannon's hand finally slipped out of his, 'that whenever that boy comes into my shop, it's on the house. Anything that boy wants is on the house. Saveloy, large haddock, cod, plaice, pies, pickled eggs, the works. Curry sauce isn't a problem and he can have as much pop as he pleases. Now, I can't say fairer than that, can I Shan?'

Over the light-flecked crowd, a red rocket arced towards the old community centre. 'Ahhhhhh...,' gasped the company.

Heads turned as the rocket hit brick and, still thrusting, began to descend down the wall. A second later it exploded, lighting up part of the windowless complex of buildings with orange effulgence. A runt of a cheer rippled through the crowd.

Greg was stood away, watching. In each hand was a hotdog without mustard.

'Freebies from Chippy Chips, eh?' said Shannon. 'Haven't heard that one before.'

James chuckled at the shared joke, but saw the barb underneath. She wasn't softened just yet.

'Does the boy need a job? I could use some help at Chippy Chips if he was up for it. Make it a family business, like.'

Above, a fist of light flicked out a hot pink peony of fingers.

'What did you just say?' said Shannon.

James blinked at her. 'What?'

Shannon was shouting now. In his face. Screaming now. Up and in his face, a single breath taking her.

'What did you fucking say to me? What the fuck did you fucking say to me you fucking prick, you fucking horrible fucking prick? You merciless fucking horrible fucking prick you go and you fucking die. You go and you fucking crawl into that shit shop hole you own. You'll never fucking have him because he's never been fucking yours. He's mine! You understand that? He's fucking fucking mine he is! Mine!'

Despite the noise around them, Shannon had drawn a little crowd. A sparkler was running down close to the nibs of a child's fingers. A bonfire of eyes was on them.

James had recoiled during her explosion, but now he leaned back in toward her, into her, breath searing and breath cold. 'I lied you know,' he said, 'I did call you a munter. And a slag. Would fuck anyone for a packet of soggy bloody chips.'

And then James turned around and shoved his way into the pile of packed bodies, which soon swallowed him. Shannon scanned her spectators, peppering them with the sparks of her hatred.

Then she turned away from the audience, away from the display and towards the white boxes that edged the field.

She found him by a van. The hotdogs were gone and his face was down into his coat and fixed on his phone. Bernard was nowhere to be seen. He seemed startled when Shannon caught him by the shoulders. She was out of breath and the blue wheel of her irises seared at him.

'You are not like that man,' she gasped, 'You're a Nacullian.

Do you know what that means, Greg? Do you?'

And then she embraced him and began to weep, with great convulsions Greg had never felt through him before. He looked around quickly, but no one was watching them. Greg slowly raised his arms around Shannon and moved them awkwardly up and down his mother's form. Inside the cordon of her son's arms, Greg could hear her, muffled and mewing, repeating her words, repeating them, each time with less energy.

'Yeah Mum,' said Greg, 'I know what it means.'

But he didn't know what it meant.

CHAPTER TWENTY-FOUR

The Sin-Eater
(2019)

No clocks ticked as Greg arrived home, because the house had only digital clocks, with their quiet and implacable timekeeping. These clocks went beep on the hour, but Greg did not always notice this.

He had become hot on the short walk home, because it was summer and Greg always walked quickly, there being little to see between work and the flat but the road which lead into the city's centre. As he came through the door he unpeeled his black patent shoes and tubed up his navy work sweater over his head, which was then flung down on the beige hallway floor.

There was no food in the house, and Greg was hungry after his long shift. This was why he had brought back the needed ingredients. It was always this way. With his staff discount, Greg would buy food for 24 hours, and then after, the house would be empty again, and he would go out again.

Inside a battered bag-for-life were the items he had purchased with that 10% discount. The list was this: a small loaf of white farmhouse bread dusted with flour, a small packet of salted Irish butter, a bottle of dark ale, a small block of cheddar, vintage. He placed the bag on the sideboard in the same place he always did, next to the white cooker with its black gas rings.

This was the way of things. In the kitchenette, the cupboards were clean of food and the fridge sat unhumming under the faux-marble worktop. A kettle, unscaled by the hard water of the city, stood next to two lozenge-shaped shakers of salt and pepper, half empty or full, as befits preference. Next to them, an old cream microwave was unplugged. Cups and crockery and cutlery and glasses and utensils were in the drawers and the alcoves and the places they had always been. Greg took down one large white plate and one dinner knife for the butter and cheese. From a different drawer, he removed a longer knife to cut the bread. He turned around and placed them on the table, where they had been many times before.

The window looked out onto the busyish road, one of the minor limbs to and from the east of the city. Inside, the sun sat square on the kitchen table, soundless and expected and at home, like the lightest of pets. Greg put himself down on one of the two chairs and waited a moment, enjoying the slow cooling of his body and of being at the expected place at the expected time.

He stared down at himself. His nipples were small, ruddy things that each sported a little crop circle of wiry black hair. The fat of his chest had pursed the nipples into mild ovals, but Greg could remember when they had started to appear rounder. His stomach, large and pale, was fronded with a delicate whiteish down; a lover's detail. When he looked down at his body in this way, Greg always noticed that he was not just a pale man, but a white man too, though he did not know if this meant something to him or meant nothing at all.

A truck passing outside disturbed the light on the table, and

Greg shifted in his chair. Somewhere, he could feel an ache. Not the ache that comes from lifting three-dozen cans of corned beef to the top self, or the ache that comes from bending down to replace economy baked beans at the bottom shelf, but a more integral ache, deep behind his spine. Perhaps he had been sleeping awkwardly of late, or maybe it was something in his diet, or something not in his diet.

Greg got up and transferred the bag-for-life from the worktop to the table. Gradually, the food was laid out, piece by piece, in the square of sunlight on the table's surface. He nudged the bread a little to the right and the butter a little to the left. He stood back to see, and then moved forward to straighten the bread knife. Then everything was in its place, and Greg took a moment to notice that everything was.

Yes, there was an order to things: A slice would be cut, the slice would be buttered, the cheese would be cut, the cheese placed on the bread. This was the way. Then a bite, two bites, and then a long glug of bottled ale. Though he was hungry, he ate gradually, quietly and implacably, because this was where he should have been, and this was what he should be doing.

Greg raised the brown glass of the bottle to his mouth and tilted it, keeping his head straight as he drank. The ale was sun-warmed and sticky, hop-bitter and malt-sweet. In one of the kitchen cupboards Greg had an oak tankard he had bought on a trip to Chepstow Castle three years ago. He had gone there with her, for her birthday. He sometimes considered filling this tankard with ale and watching as the head rose fizzing to the rounded rim. Though no one would see if he did, he was worried that it seemed pretentious somehow. After all, he was always watching himself, like everyone was.

A slice was cut, the slice was buttered. The cheese was cut, then placed on the bread. Then a bite, two bites, and a long glug of the ale. This was the way, the gathering and ebbing of the meal. This had to be continued, because if it did not continue, then the meal would never be finished, not properly finished.

Outside the flat, the light was marbling into evening proper. Somewhere, a line had been crossed and the city had begun to give up the heat it had hoarded throughout the day. Though no one could see it, great thermals were rising into the city's sky and above, some birds that few people knew the name of screamed to one other in a barrel of warm, rising air. Down in the small white office above the supermarket, Greg's manager was checking over employee timesheets and was wishing she could go home. And at her home, another woman was putting a bottle of white wine into a fridge, wishing she had been more adventurous than pinot grigio.

A slice, a buttered slice. Some cheese, cheese on bread. A bite, two bites. Then a draught of ale. This was the way. He was two thirds through the loaf now. In truth, Greg had passed by his hunger some time ago, but he ate on anyway, because this was where he should have been and this was what he should be doing. The butter was the most difficult thing, because there was always too much of it and the more he ate, the richer it seemed on his tongue and in his stomach. But the thought of binning it or saving it for tomorrow was impossible, Greg knew that.

There was one hunk of bread left now, a tapering beige crust that had lost its dusting of flour as Greg had cut the loaf into uneven slices. With his knife he lifted the soft yellow wedge of butter and placed it at one end of the bread's white surface. He spread out the butter, a centimetre thick, over the slice. Then with the knife, he cut through the remaining cheese, making two thick slabs, which flaked slightly at the edges. He placed the cheese on the bread, sinking the slabs into the butter, which spread out sideways in gentle fatty waves. A bite, two bites. Then a draught of ale. And again. And repeat.

Greg was chewing and looking down at the table's surface. The square of light had shifted away now and could not be seen. This was always the way. To his left, back in the hallway, a coat that was not his remained on a hook. It was purple and puffy and had fake fur edging around the heavy hood. It was hung next to his black raincoat, which he had not used in some time, because he didn't mind walking back in the rain. At the back end of the flat there was a room that was not his, a room that squatting and replete, remained. Greg had had no reason to go in there for some time.

He swallowed, and felt the tanned crust's edge as it went down his throat. Outside there was a road and a column of warm air and there were birds few knew the name of. There were many other things too, there simply must have been. Greg leaned back and let out a soft burp, flabby and creamy and unnoticed.

The meal was now done with, and the evening was there in front of him, quiet and implacable.

Acknowledgements

Sean Campbell, for showing me that a couple of scattered ideas was in fact a novel. Without his confidence in me, there simply would not have been a book. Editors never get the credit they deserve, so I say now that he has been a collaborator.

To the readers from Epoque; Melanie, Shan and Louise, who helped shape the invaluable editorial responses and guidance to the various drafts of this work.

To Kerrie, for reading the earliest drafts and knowing the flicksy-flocksy, sharp jabber of my style. Many improvements and ideas I owe to her.

To Cherry Smyth, who knows the meaning of kindness and integrity, in all realms.

To the Tyrone Guthrie Centre, where I took some first steps.

To Jess Moriarty, whose help as a friend and colleague will never go unpraised.

To Ross and Jenni, for giving me things that have helped keep me steady in unsteady times.

To Karis and Hu, in whose presence I always feel at home and refreshed.

To Daisy and Orlando, because they wonder and wander and always will.

To Matt and Holly, who I miss.

To Peter and Lisa, who have acted as my artistic family for many years now.

And to my mother, Sandra Jordan. She read to me as a baby, she was willing to listen and understand an odd child and she taught me that being kind was not a weakness. She stopped me from going insane, when I was very young. She missed meals to feed me, she begged others to stop me from being expelled. She did not love authority, but she respected skill. She was very imperfect, but she did not wish to be imperfect.